GENTLY IN THE SUN

Every man in Hiverton knows Rachel Campion. She is the most gorgeous girl to have turned up in the fishing village in living memory. When she is discovered lying dead on the beach, Gently joins the throngs of summer visitors on their annual pilgrimage to the seaside in the midst of a summer heatwave – and as the temperature soars, the mystery deepens. The long-buried skeleton of a woman is unearthed close to where Rachel's body was found and Gently suddenly has the riddle of two mysterious deaths to solve.

GENTLY IN THE SUN

by

Alan Hunter

Magna Large Print Books
Long Preston, North Yorkshire,
BD23 4ND, England.

British Library Cataloguing in Publication Data.

Hunter, Alan
    Gently in the sun.

    A catalogue record of this book is
    available from the British Library

    ISBN   978-0-7505-3496-3

First published in Great Britain in 1959

Published in Large Print 2012 by arrangement with
Constable & Robinson Ltd.

Magna Large Print is an imprint of Library Magna Books Ltd.

Printed and bound in Great Britain by
T.J. (International) Ltd., Cornwall, PL28 8RW

CHAPTER ONE

Even at this hour in the morning, when the dew still clung heavily to the rough, wiry blades of the marram, one could tell that by early afternoon the temperature would be nearing ninety. The sky stretched arching from the sea horizon like pale porcelain. The fawn sand, moist on the surface, kicked up underfoot as though it were parched brown sugar. Inland, beyond the red-brick cluster of the village, a field of beet looked bluish between straw-coloured acres; the field oaks were stringy and slanted by the wind; they made dark, heavy patches of unrelieved colour. In Hiverton itself there were no trees. One saw them only on rising ground to the south. There the Bel-Air guest house peered blandly at the North Sea, its numerous windows a-sparkle in the sunlight.

Another burning day was in prospect, turning the beach into a gridiron, the village into an oven! Already the sun was becoming spiteful and shortening its track on the steel-blue sea. Grasshoppers had begun to buzz too early, the larks were tired of their morning song. Soon one would see the visitors come straggling across the marrams, their brightly coloured towels slung over their shoulders. The tide which had brought in the longshore boats was ebbing away to make sport for the bathers.

Just now there was only a single figure on the marram hills, a solitary man followed by a solitary dog. The man wore a shapeless brown jacket, sagged at the corners; the dog, a supple, yellowish beast, slunk along close to his heel. They both of them had a cautious air as though a sudden movement would send them scurrying. The man nursed something straight under the left side of his jacket, and the dog, occasionally, passed a pink tongue round its muzzle.

'Come you on, blast you!'

The dog had turned aside for a moment: it wanted to investigate one of the lizards which frequented the marrams.

'Do you want to get me hung?'

It jumped away, its mouth twitching. After a couple of reluctant frisks it was back again at heel.

A short distance from the fishermen's net store the man halted abruptly. In a small hill-top depression before him was pitched a

8

khaki-coloured tent. A bicycle lay beside it, and, near the flaps, some aluminium utensils. A sea-scrubbed bough had been lugged up from the beach and pressed into service as draining board and general furniture.

The man ran his eye over it, stock-still, listening. There was no movement in the tent, but that didn't mean to say...

'Cubbo, boy, cubbo!'

With a muttered word, he slid down the hillside. His descent put up some sandpipers, but the dog made no attempt to spring at them.

'Good little old boy – cubbo!'

Together they plodded through the yielding sand. Ahead of them now lay the fishermen's boats, seven or eight strung out in a line. Round about them was strewn wet seaweed from the nets and one could see the fresh tracks where the boats had been winched up the beach. Already, no doubt, at the fish market in Starmouth.

'What's the matter, boy? What d'you see?'

The dog had stopped, its hackles rising. Crouching back in the sand it was trembling and snarling, its teeth revealed under a curling lip. Alerted, the man clutched his gun closer to his body, but he could hear no sound and detect no movement.

'What's the matter, you stupid so-and-so–?'

The dog increased its snarls, its muzzle pointing towards the boats.

'There's nothing there, you fule!'

He could swear they were alone on the beach. The fishermen were in bed and Mears, the constable, on his beat. That beat, he well knew, took the policeman to West Somerby crossroads. Not once in ten years at this time in the morning...

He edged closer to the boats. The dog whined like a thing possessed. Snuffling and scolding, it dug in its feet and refused point blank to follow him. There was something uncanny about its behaviour: all the hair down its back had lifted. Its beady eyes were beseeching him in an ecstasy of dumb terror.

With an oath he strode over to the boats, determined to know one way or the other. Lying at all angles just as they had been left, they presented almost at a glance their innocency of occupants. And yet that confounded dog ... in a minute somebody would hear him!

And then the man, too, started back in the sugary sand. A look of bemused incredulity crept over his coarse features. Between two of the boats ... only part of it showing... He swallowed once or twice without even closing his mouth.

'Cubbo, boy–!'

He began to run heavily up the beach. The dog, flying ahead, was barking as though to wake the houses. Over the gap and down the track he pounded, cursing as he felt the bouncing gun. It had to be him who stumbled into it, his pockets filled from a successful morning!

Fortunately, the village was to all appearances deserted. Only Mrs Neal was about, taking in the Beach Stores' bundle of papers.

'What's up with that dog, Fred ... can't you keep it from barking?'

Breathlessly he plunged into the shop with its mingled smell of apples and bacon.

'First take these blessed things off me!'

Out came the gun and half a dozen fat rabbits. Before the astonished woman could protest, they were loaded into her arms.

'Now get on the telephone – ring up Ferrety Mears! There's a dead woman down on the beach – it's that fancy piece from the guest house. Dead as a nit, I tell you, and not wearing nothing to talk about!'

He clawed for a moment at the sweat which was trickling down his face. Then, probably feeling that ceremony was pointless, he drew himself a glass of orange squash.

The sun was a little higher when Constable Mears strode over the gap. Above the hills the air had started to tremble and the sea looked darker below them. Small blue butterflies played over the grass tufts, their colours bleached by the brilliant light; along the tideline terns were dipping, and further out a school of gulls.

It was still quite early, but not early enough. The Hiverton grapevine had already been in action. About the handful of boats had gathered a mixed crowd of people – half dressed, some of them, the fishermen tousled and unwashed. They stood in silent groups in the presence of the dead. A shuffled foot or an uneasy mutter was all one heard above the wash of the sea.

'Get back there, some of you!'

Mears's angry order sounded out of place. Resentfully they turned to stare at him and his delegated authority. Wasn't he just one of themselves, though masquerading in a uniform?

'These kids about here ... haven't you got any sense?'

Two of the men, visitors, were shamed into calling away their offspring.

The sand was dry now and almost the

colour of platinum. The shadows of the boats fell across it sharp and hard. Like sections of exotic fruit the boats lay shoulder to shoulder, their gay colours explosive under the white fire of the sun.

'You was it who found it?'

Nockolds, with Neal from the store, was on guard. To help preserve the decencies they had brought down some potato sacks. Nockolds was in his shirtsleeves: he had thought it prudent to shed his poacher's jacket.

'About half-an-hour ago.'

'On your own were you?'

'I ran all the way.'

'Hold these sacks up, will you? We don't want everyone...'

Between them they made some sort of a screen, and Mears was enabled to view the body. It was of a woman in her late twenties, and she had been outstandingly beautiful. She had long, jet-black hair and a bold, heart-shaped face, but the former was now soiled with sand and the latter convulsed and bluish. She lay stiffly on her back and was wearing only crimson beach pyjamas. The jacket was undone revealing pale, shapely breasts. It also revealed two livid bruises, one on each side of her throat. The body was rigid and the pyjamas damp with dew.

'Touch her, did you?'

'Not blessed likely!'

Mears stooped to feel her wrist but was repelled by its chilly stiffness. In between the boats it was still cold and shadowed. The seaweed lying there remained limp and fresh-smelling.

'What time did the boats come in?'

''Bout four ... thereabouts.'

'She wasn't there then?'

'Blast no, do we'd have said something!'

'Anyone recognize her?'

That was an easy one. All the men in the village had kept an eye on this beauty.

'She come from the guest house.'

'Rachel – that's what her name is!'

'Been here above a week...'

'She never wore more than...'

Mears took out his notebook and began to scribble it down. A few of the bolder ones were trying to peep between the boats, but Nockolds and Neal held their sacks together jealously. All the time newcomers came hastening down from the gap.

'What time did you finish here?'

'Getting on for half past five.'

'See anyone about then?'

'Not a soul bar us lot.'

'How many of you went out last night?'

All of them, it appeared, who had a boat or a share in one. The moon was coming to its full and the longshore fishing was profitable. With a good catch they had returned in the brooding light of the dawn; the boats had been hauled up, the fish unloaded into baskets, and the nets carried up to dry at the store. Then they had tumbled into bed leaving the boats to throw long shadows...

'Had Mason gone off with the fish?'

'Blast yes, before we'd got the nets away.'

'Who was the last to leave?'

They were three of the elder men and they had left all together.

Now the bystanders were more talkative, some of their tongues having been loosened. The visitors in particular were excitedly canvassing each other's opinions. For them it wasn't so serious, if anything rather an event. A couple of teenagers were staying at the Bel-Air, and they were assiduous in their efforts to peer round the sacks.

'The doctor is on his way ... can I trust you two?'

Mears was putting away his notebook and frowning at the curious assembly. He would liked to have cleared the beach but was aware of his limited authority.

'Nobody's to touch anything ... they're to

15

keep out of the boats.'

He stumped away looking fierce and flustered. They would blame him, but what could one man do? Behind him, before he had got a dozen yards, he could hear the shuffle of encroaching feet. If by chance there had happened to be some clues about...

He resisted temptation and didn't turn his head.

In effect his departure had a dampening influence on the sightseers. Their huddling forward was a herd-movement and not the pursuit of curiosity. Mears had acted as a catalyst. His presence had made them vocal. Now, the most bold among them had become the most silent.

'He's gone to ring up the C.I.D.'

It was only by degrees that the affair crept into perspective. In a little while what was almost private would become the property of the public.

'The press'll be here soon, you see.'

'The Sunday papers...'

'Do you reckon they'll call in?'

For the tenth time Nockolds dashed the sweat from his face. Dimly he could begin to see that there was trouble building up for him. He'd kept telling himself a story about a walk to exercise his dog, but the more he turned it over the less likely did it seem. Mears might have accepted it, but after Mears were coming other people...

'You're sure it's that black-haired mawther?'

Bob Hawks, the mean-faced owner of the *Boy Cyril*, had arrived too late to get a glimpse of the exhibit.

'Let's have a look, Fred – just a quick 'un!'

But Fred, with a guilty conscience, was permitting quick looks to no man.

Now they could hear the doctor's car pulling up with a skirmish of brakes. Doctor Banning was a young man who had only just begun to practise. His passing likeness to Jeff Chandler had spread epidemics among his female clients.

'Good lord, have you no respect for the dead!'

One had to admire his cool manner and the authority of his boyish voice. Without exerting himself he got the crowd to move off – further, indeed, than Mears had done.

'Now, let's see.'

He was down on his knees without turning a hair.

Hawks, still hovering close, peered shamelessly over the doctor's shoulder. His dark-brown eyes glittered and an odd expression showed on his long thin face.

'Get you back, Bob!'

Nockolds nudged him, but Hawks didn't seem to notice. He watched fascinated while the doctor's hands ran tentatively over the stiffened body. For no reason at all a child had begun to bawl its head off, while up on the marrams, not far from the net store, appeared the young man whose tent had diverted the poacher.

'Bring plenty of screens,' Mears was advising the County H.Q.

Near his phone box a wall thermometer was already registering seventy-six.

By ten that evening the temperature was still in the seventies. All along the road to Wendham, where the County Constabulary had its headquarters, Inspector Dyson had been passing pubs outside which shirt-sleeved men were standing with glasses. At Strawsett there had been some dancing. A youth in a singlet was bouncing a scarlet accordion. From the wide-open windows of stuffy bedrooms children, unable to sleep, had waved listlessly at the passing police car.

At Wendham it was just the same, the narrow streets alive with people. In sleeveless shirts and dresses they sauntered aimlessly

18

in the twilight. Around the market-cross some kids were screaming, their limbs and faces tanned as brown as nuts. High above, in the pale sky, swifts were circling on thin crescent wings.

'Will you want the car again, sir?'

Dyson made a face as he slammed the door. He had caught the sun badly on his face and arms and tomorrow, he knew from experience, his nose would peel like a burst tomato. But most of all he was wanting a pint of beer. The idea had tantalized him all the way from Hiverton. During the whole wearisome day, beginning at eight o'clock that morning, nothing had gratified his thirst except ice cream and cups of tea.

'The super is waiting for you upstairs.'

Neither, in fact, had he eaten much either.

'This afternoon the C.C. was here.'

'Tell them to send me up some coffee and sandwiches, will you?'

Superintendent Stock had followed the current fashion of undress. He was sitting in his shirtsleeves and had removed both shoes and socks. An electric fan buzzed at the corner of his desk; he was nursing, with little enthusiasm, a glass of canteen lemonade.

'My God, what a scorcher it's been!'

There were times when even homicide

19

had to take second place.

'You'd think, out there at the coast...'

'It couldn't have been hotter than it's been in Wendham.'

Dyson sat, spreading his legs. Perhaps it was a shower he needed most! He felt in his pocket for his cigarettes, then changed his mind in a wave of loathing. The super waited patiently, tipping his glass now and then.

'I can't see us making an early arrest.'

'That's what I was afraid of ... I had to admit it to the C.C.'

'Her boss, or whatever he is, he seems the best bet. But there's nothing to tie him in, nor the young fellow either. Or six or seven others who had been making passes at her.'

'Like that, was it?'

'She was a pin-up all right.'

'Let's go over the ground carefully.'

Dyson nodded, raking at his sodden shirt.

'Rachel Campion, single, age twenty-eight, resident at West Hampstead for the past two years. According to this Mixer, she'd been his private secretary, but he doesn't seem to know a lot about her antecedents. They arrived at the Bel-Air guest house last Saturday week. They had adjacent rooms and were staying a fortnight. Campion made a big splash with all the males in the place, and she was seen in the company of a young fellow called Simmonds. He calls himself a painter and is camping on the marrams.

'Last night there was a filmshow at the next village, Hamby. Most of the guests went to it in transport provided by the guest house. They left at six-thirty and arrived back at about eleven-fifteen, but Mixer didn't go with them and neither did Campion. Mixer says he went to Starmouth to see a show on the pier. He was driving his own car and left the guest house at six-twenty. They'd given him a door key so that he could let himself in, and the bartender vouches that he was back soon after midnight.

'Campion, on the other hand, spent the evening at the guest house. She was there for dinner and had a drink at half past nine. After that nobody saw her again, but the impression is that she went to her room. During the evening she was wearing the beach-pyjamas in which she was found later.

'At midnight the fishing boats put out, and returned at around four a.m. The men were busy unloading and getting their nets out until approximately five-thirty. At just after seven the local poacher found Campion's body. It was lying partly hidden between two of the boats. Mears, the village constable, saw it at seven-thirty-five: he made a note of the fact that the pyjamas were damp, which suggests that the body had been exposed all night.

'The medical report–' Dyson paused. 'I expect you've seen it. She probably wasn't raped, though she'd been with a man not long before. Death was effected by strangulation. The strangulation was violent. She was killed around midnight, roughly between eleven p.m. and one a.m. Some of the nails are bent back but nothing useful has been recovered from them.

'Those are the principal facts that have come to light today. As I said, an early arrest doesn't seem very likely.'

'Hmm.'

The super twisted his empty glass between his fingers. In spite of the fan, there was a gleam of sweat on his forehead. A constable with his collar undone brought in a tray with Dyson's sandwiches. Through the open window came the noise of traffic in the High Street.

'There's a number of interesting points there, Dyson.'

Dyson ate without appetite, grunting when he tasted the coffee.

'In the first place, where was the body all

night? and why did someone get up early to put it where it was found?'

'I've been thinking about that.'

'Then this other point ... about the man.'

'It struck me directly I saw the report.'

'Perhaps you'd better give me your ideas.'

Illogically, it seemed to Dyson that the fan was stealing his air. He got up and took his tray to the illusive relief of the thrown-up window. Outside it was nearly dark. A violet tint had deepened the sky. The super had switched on his desk lamp soon after Dyson had entered the office.

'Doesn't it look like a *crime passionel?* All the makings are there, I'd say! An attractive woman – her jealous boss – several interested males – and now this medical evidence. Mixer found her with a bloke when he came back from Starmouth ... and there you are. That's how I see it.'

'He admits she was his mistress?'

'Naturally not! But he's lying his head off. A business man doesn't take a poppet like that on vacation for nothing.'

'What's he like, this Mixer chap?'

'A flashy type; a bit of a spiv.'

'What's his business?'

'Company promoting – which could mean anything under the sun. He gives a business address in the City ... possibly Records could tell us something.'

The super nodded sagely.

'He seems to fit the bill. What about the bloke she was with – any idea who he might have been?'

'That's the trouble. It might have been anyone.'

'What about Simmonds?'

'I gave him a grilling. He admitted he'd spoken to her on the beach once or twice, but I'd heard that up at the guest house already.'

'Was he lying, do you think?'

'He was nervous. I couldn't tell.'

'And you questioned some of the others?'

'Four or five of them at the guest house. But it adds up the same way – none of them will admit anything. And you can't narrow it down to Simmonds and the guest house.'

Dyson gulped some of his vile coffee and reached for another sandwich. Only one thing mattered in this business, he knew. He had put it first: no arrest was imminent. Once you'd said that the rest was very largely...

'Well, I suppose it's not important, though it might have helped the case. What was your idea about the body being left outside all night?'

'It's to do with the tide, I think. He was

going to dump it in the sea.'

'How did the tide affect that?'

'It was flooding when he got down there. As I see it he made his first attempt soon after he did the murder. He drove the body down to the beach but found the fishermen there launching their boats. So he parked it somewhere handy – that accounts for the damp pyjamas. Later on, when he tried again, the tide was flooding and he'd lost his chance.'

'So he left it by the boats.'

'You have to remember that it was daylight. He probably came on foot, and a body is heavy in any case.'

The super massaged his chin with fingers that were moist.

His beard, he noticed, felt scruffier in hot weather than at other times.

'You checked his car, I suppose?'

'It's a Citroen. It was clean enough.'

'Anyone see it or hear it at the relevant times?'

'Nobody I've questioned yet.'

'So in fact you've got nothing material against him?'

Dyson shrugged feebly. Hadn't he said as much?

'He fits the pattern and that's about all – apart from that it might have been anyone.'

'Anyone at all who was jealous enough to murder.'

The super sighed regretfully. 'You see where it gets us. Unless we can show something quick I daren't hang on to the case. I talked to the C.C. I asked him for a couple of days at least. Between you and me this heat makes him irritable.'

'We aren't homicide experts.'

'That's just what he's been telling me. I'm afraid you've had this one, Dyson, unless you can suggest something else.'

Dyson finished his coffee in silence. He had had a presentment of the outcome all day. At one point in the afternoon, when he had been questioning Mixer, he had realized with a bitter clarity that he was straying out of his depth. For homicide you needed a specialist: one couldn't be two people.

'On the whole it would be a relief.'

The super nodded at the flickering fan-blades.

'We don't see much of homicide, not enough to signify.'

'It's the only way to look at it, Dyson. Murder's an unreasonable responsibility.'

'And in this weather too! Anyone can have it, for me.'

Above the roofs now a moon was rising, a

26

fisherman's moon. It lay big and pale over the housetops of Wendham. At Hiverton it would be looking down on seven boats on an empty beach. And soon would come the fishermen with their nets over their shoulders.

CHAPTER TWO

It was the eighth day of the heat wave, and hotter than it had ever been. The sun was like a baleful presence nailed to a merciless sky. With both windows down the train compartment had been sweltering, and here and there, beside the track, one had seen black patches of spark-ignited grass. Gently, who never stood on ceremony, had stripped to his braces before the train reached Chelmsford. At Norchester Thorpe he had dived through the barrier for a hasty glass of beer. It had tasted insipid and only made him sweat the more, while Dutt, sprawled in his seat, seemed to have remained the cooler of the two.

'But when we get to the sea...'

That was what he had kept telling himself. In his mind's eye he had seen the pastelled marrams stir in the breeze. And the sea it-self, the long falling combers; once get down to that and it would have to be cooler!

Only at Hamby there was no sea to be seen, and certainly nothing suggestive of a breeze. The little station lay blistering in a heat still untempered, its asphalt platform soft to the foot. The porter, who picked up their bags, shed sweat. His face was the colour of a freshly boiled lobster.

'But when we get to the sea...'

It couldn't be so far away. Beyond the line of dusty trees, perhaps, beyond the air danc-ing over the pantiles.

'*Morning Chronicle* – can you give us a statement?'

They had warned him that the press was taking a keen interest in the affair. A reporter in a printed play shirt was shoving a note-book under Gently's nose, while in the back-ground a photographer manoeuvred for a shot.

'As you see, we've just arrived.'

'Have the police got a theory?'

'It was probably a man who did it.'

'Hasn't Mixer been inside?'

'If you check the records...'

'Isn't it a fact that she was his mistress?'

A thin-faced man with prominent teeth

hurried up just as the photographer was immortalizing Gently's *déshabille*.

'Sorry I'm late ... the car broke down! It's all right now, I've got it outside.'

'Are we fixed up at the Bel-Air?'

'Yes, but it wasn't easy. They've had to turn two of the staff out of their rooms.'

He had met Dyson before, about six months previously. The county man wasn't really surprised to see Gently in braces and trailing his jacket. The photographer, however, couldn't get enough of it. He ran ahead into the station yard and took two more candid shots.

'Was it like this in town?'

Above the bonnet of the police Wolseley the air simmered as though the engine was boiling. When you opened a door the heat spilled out, carrying along with it a smell of warm leather.

'Yesterday it was ninety-one. Today, so they tell me...'

Steeling himself, Gently plunged into the oven-like interior.

Once they were moving things became more tolerable. The air that rushed in wasn't cool but it was moving. They were driving through flat country along a narrow coastal road. To the right, although the sea was invisible, one could see the pale marram hills which marked the boundary of the land.

'We sent you the file by despatch.'

'I looked it over coming up.'

'Naturally, with only one day...'

'I thought you'd done a pretty sound job.'

Dyson looked relieved rather than pleased. He was driving, Gently noticed, with text-book care and attention.

'What about the photographs?'

'You'll find some in that briefcase.'

'I want to know what this Campion looked like before she was killed.'

'There's a couple there I got from Mixer. He was carrying them about in his pocket.'

Gently delved in the briefcase, pausing only briefly over the official post-mortem photographs. The two which had belonged to Mixer were post-card enlargements a little soiled at the edges. One was a full-length and the other a three-quarter profile. The full-length print showed the victim in a bikini.

'Some dish, wasn't she?'

Dyson threw Gently a curious side glance.

'From what I've been hearing she was everything she looks. She made a stir in Hiverton during the short time she was there.'

'Went round with several men, did she?'

'No, but not because they didn't try!'

'Because her boss kept an eye on her?'

'You'll never get him to say so.'

Gently held the two photographs side by side, staring from one to the other. A 'brunette bombshell' was how one of the morning papers had described her. Slender, rather tall, she had the feline type of gracefulness. Her bust and hips were large and there was a misting of down on her calves. Her features were strong and the nose a little prominent. Her black hair, perfectly straight, flowed down her back like the mane of a horse. But it was the eyes that held the secret, the pulsating key to the woman. They were large and very dark and set a long way apart. They didn't have a smile, and neither did the ripe-lipped mouth. Instead they suggested a smile, a smile compact of sensual intelligence: in a moment one seemed to have penetrated all the promise of the passionate body.

'Do you think he'd introduce her to his wife?'

Gently grunted and dropped the photographs back into the briefcase. They had come to a string of houses reaching out down the dusty road; just beyond them, at a crossing, was the flint tower of an enormous church.

'Is this the village?'

'Yes ... this is Hiverton.'

Dyson turned off right by the church. The village street down which they cruised was short and disappointingly commonplace, and was flanked by flint cobble cottages and featureless houses of local brick. The church had promised something better, but one looked in vain for a compensating factor.

'The Bel-Air is to the right – over there, amongst those trees.'

Dyson paused at a lop-sided crossways for Gently to take it in.

'To the left you might call it residential – some rows of old terrace houses! Straight ahead is the track across the marrams. The boats are pulled up on the far side of the gap.'

'What's that hut place by the gap?'

'It belongs to the fishermen, I believe.'

'And that other thing, on stilts?'

'A coastguard lookout, but it's disused these days.'

Really, there was nothing to see in Hiverton! Dyson pressed the accelerator with gentle impatience. But Gently was still gazing about at the sun-struck scene, unconscious, apparently, of the rising temperature in the car.

'Let's stop at that shop with the grass hats

hung outside.'

Dyson let in his clutch with a suspicion of a jerk.

'I've questioned the fellow there, but I'm pretty sure he doesn't know.'

'I'm too hot to talk shop! What I want are some of those play shirts.'

Leaving Dyson with Dutt in the car he went up the steps of the establishment. It was a modern shop with two long counters and seemed to sell everything from slabcake to paperbacks. A bright-faced woman in overalls was making ice cream cornets for two children. She gave Gently a smile and blew expressively through rounded lips.

'Anyway, it's good for trade – that's what I say!'

He bought three of the shirts of the sort he had seen the reporter wearing. They were manufactured in Hong Kong and not very expensive. One of them was printed with rich fruit-like designs in green, orange, purple, and black, another featured rock-and-roll singers, the third film actresses. If that photographer really wanted something to enliven the silly season!

'I'd better have a hat – one of those Italian straws with the green bands. And a pair of sunglasses. Have you sandals in a broad nine fitting?'

He finished up with a bottle of sun lotion and a threepenny ice cream cornet. Nibbling at the latter he began to feel happier, in spite of the intolerable heat. He had been given the run of the shop. The proprietress was treating him almost like an acquaintance. As he had pondered the various items she had left him for other customers, returning each time with a fresh smile and a remark.

'You're popular here, I see.'

'We do our best to keep people happy.'

'Where's your husband today?'

'Do you want him? He's having his lunch with the girl.'

For some reason he was wanting to linger there: it was as though, quite by accident, he had got his foot in at Hiverton. The Beach Stores, it was obvious, played a big part in the village scene. People came there to exchange a word as well as to make their purchases.

'Did you get what you wanted?'

Dyson couldn't help the sarcasm. He squirmed as he turned the Wolseley in front of the shop. His long nose was peeling and the colour of rhubarb, and he shrank every time Gently came near his arm.

They took the turning to the guest house, which passed a public house on its left. To the right were ugly bungalows of a bad pre-war vintage and, a little further on, an estate of forbidding council houses. There were no two ways about it – Hiverton was no beauty spot. It had a breathtaking church, but it had very little else.

'I expect you'll want to have a talk with Mixer.'

'To begin with I want a shower.'

'He struck me as being... I suppose you checked with Records?'

'And then something to eat. I scamped breakfast to catch the train.'

He caught a puzzled expression on the county man's face: Dyson wasn't quite used to Gently yet. He was apparently expecting him to dive straight in, armed with his particular brand of Central Office magic.

'In my report, as you've seen...'

'It was adequate, I thought.'

'Then you agree with me that Mixer?'

'What's the food like at the Bel-Air?'

Dyson sliced the car through an open pair of white gates, puffing up fiercely and with a scuttling of gravel. The Bel-Air loomed above them in Edwardian grandeur; it was marzipan and brick of the most exuberant vintage. A stopped door revealed a vista of black-and-white tiles. The sash windows were fitted with pale yellow Venetian blinds. In a room not far away someone was playing a jazz record, and one could also hear the sound of a tennis ball being struck.

If Gently had been down there on holiday he could hardly have behaved more eccentrically. That was Dyson's fixed impression by the time they had finished lunch.

Gently, resplendent in his fruity shirt, was well aware of his colleague's opinion, but he gave no sign of it as he dallied over his coffee.

They had taken the meal alone, the three of them. It was half past two and most people had retired, some of them to the beach, some to deckchairs in the garden. Six times during the past quarter of an hour Dyson had tried to get to business, and six times Gently had merely grunted and continued to stare at the pretty waitress.

Now he was just sitting there, spinning out time over the coffee. He had had his shower, he had eaten his lunch, and that seemed to be everything at present on his mind.

'How about some more coffee?'

Injuredly, Dyson poured it for him. From the way it was received he knew that Gently was stalling him. Nobody in this heat could want two cups of coffee.

As a matter of fact, Gently's state of mind was curious. Ever since he had seen the photographs his ideas had been saturated by Rachel Campion. A woman ... but what sort of woman? That was what he couldn't decide on. Again and again he had summoned the pictures before his eyes, trying to fit a character to the enigma of the flat statement.

Those eyes – was it perhaps just a trick of the camera? Were they really such windows to a world of reckless passion? And her body, too, with the perfection of imperfection: was it honestly so calculated to whet the keen edge of desire?

He would never know, he could only imagine. The reality he was left with was the garbled witness of chance observers. But he wanted to know and he kept trying to surprise the knowledge. A woman ... but what sort of a woman? Everything seemed to hang on it!

'Waitress, come here a moment.'

Her name was Rosie and she was a synthetic blonde. Her fairly obvious attractions did not go unappreciated. Gently had noticed a suggestive passage between her and Maurice, the slim young bartender.

'Was it you who waited at Miss Campion's table?'

'Oh yes – she sat at that one by the window.'

'Was she easy to get on with?'

'She wasn't a lot of trouble.'

'Tip you, did she?'

'It was her boss who did the tipping.'

'What did you think of her?'

Rosie giggled.

'She'd got what it took, but she had her head screwed on too. All the men had a spot for her, even old Colonel Morris. If you ask me, some of the wives here aren't so sorry about what's happened.'

'What do you mean by saying that she had her head screwed on?'

'She kept her eye on the main chance, that's what I mean. Her boss was jealous and she wouldn't play the fool. Mind you, I wasn't kidded. I know an act when I see one. There were times when he wasn't about and then she wasn't quite so starchy – only she never let it get anywhere, if you see what I mean. She'd got a wonderful talent for knowing where to draw a line.'

'She was what you'd call a tease?'

Rosie giggled again, but the question didn't embarrass her. At twenty-four or -five she had the assurance of a much older woman.

'I wouldn't know that, would I? But I

wouldn't put it past her. Some women get a kick out of that, and she was the right type. But she liked the rest too, don't you forget it. One woman can't keep that from another.'

'Who did she encourage?'

'She wasn't too particular.'

'Was there anyone especial?'

'If there was she was clever about it. She let old Colonel Morris kiss her. Then she put some of the kids into a trance. And one or two married men who ought to have known better, though it's a fact that their wives are mostly old bitches.'

'But your impression is that none of them got very far?'

'They didn't get a chance, what with her boss always hanging around.'

"What about Tuesday? He wasn't around then.'

'They'd had a row, I think, and she wasn't in the mood. In any case most of them had gone to Hamby. There were only two of the old couples playing bridge in the lounge.'

'So she spent the evening alone?'

'She was alone at dinner.'

'What about after that?'

'I went off duty. It was the last time I saw her.'

In the doorway Maurice had appeared

carrying a tray of dirty glasses. He set it down on the mahogany sideboard and began to pile on one or two more. His languorous eyes rested an instant on Rosie's trim back.

'Tell me – was she really so outstanding, or was it just her manner?'

'It was a bit of both if you ask me, but she'd got the goods in the first place.'

'Did she talk a lot, and laugh?'

'Not her. She was always serious.'

'Was she offhand to other women?'

'She could afford to be nice to them. She'd got them all whacked.'

'And how about you – weren't you jealous?'

Her giggle was accompanied by a slight gesture of the hips.

'I get along. I wasn't worried. Some gentlemen prefer blondes.'

In the glass at the back of the sideboard Maurice was now studying her profile. He had abandoned his stacked tray and was apparently counting the serviettes.

Gently stirred at last, to Dyson's great relief. He wandered out on to the verandah and stood gazing down at the afternoon sea. Below the lawn there were two hard courts for the use of the guests, and in spite of the temperature they were occupied by sweating youngsters in shorts and singlets. In the shade of the oak trees sat their elders, sleeping or knitting. From the other side of the marram hills could be heard the faint cries of children.

'I've used the reading-room for interrogation.'

Gently shrugged his multi-coloured shoulders.

'I daresay that the manager...'

'Let's take a stroll along the beach, shall we?'

It was no use, Gently would have his way. He kept bulldozing aside all Dyson's hints and veiled suggestions. He had dressed like a holidaymaker and now it seemed he was going to behave like one. With Dutt trailing behind they crossed the lawn at a leisurely saunter.

'How does one get down to the beach?'

A few of the lotus-eaters in the deckchairs looked up as they passed. They knew Dyson, of course, but they knew nothing of Gently. Superintendent Stock had carefully delayed the news that the Yard was being called in.

'Down there, past the tennis courts.'

The way led through a dusty shrubbery. At the bottom there was a gate with a spring giving access to the back of the marrams. Everything one touched was burning to the

41

hand, and the ground struck hot through the soles of shoes. The marram grass, pale and rustling, looked as though it had been dried in a botanical press.

'You can see what it's like for footprints.'

Gently nodded, plodding through the scalding sand. Still that silent face was haunting him, charging every step with its presence. Hadn't she come this way, perhaps, not much more than thirty-six hours ago? When the sand, now hot, was already cold, and the dew falling chill on the sere of the marram?

He had propped the photograph against his mirror and kept his eyes on it while he was dressing. After reading Dyson's report he had been certain that the face would tell him something. Several things might have happened. It depended upon the type of woman. Once you had settled that, then you could begin to see your way.

Only the face had told him nothing of those things he wanted to know. The obvious thing was unimportant. Even Dyson could hardly have missed it.

'There's Mixer over there now.'

They had got to the top of the hills. Below them, a steep slide, lay the silvery-fawn beach, the tiniest of combers sending white washes along its margin. The sea looked heavy and drunken with sun. Its dark acres were mottled with purple and green patches. At the tideline the children paddled and screamed, their dumpy bodies showing through their sagging swimsuits. Higher up sat the parents, some of them beneath sunshades.

'He's watching us, you bet.'

Could it even have been that passion...?

'You see? He's getting up.'

Or the body, would that tell him?

He turned impatiently in the direction which Dyson was indicating. One hadn't had to ask the county man where his suspicions lay. Alfred Joseph Mixer – he was the candidate! The 'company promoter' with his cash and cockney accent: who, in all probability, had outsmarted Dyson.

'He's expecting us to tackle him.'

Gently was only confirming impressions. In his twenty years with the Central Office he had met a lot of Mixers, and this one seemed to follow the general pattern. A biggish man of about forty with something of a stomach. Thinned hair, a large nose, and small, hard eyes. He had been sitting under a sunshade and was wearing shiny black bathing trunks. Now he was standing up apprehensively, twisting his sunglasses as he watched the three policemen.

'Don't you think perhaps?'

'What makes you so sure he did it?'

'The evidence ... well ... one forms an impression.'

'He's done time for embezzlement.'

'There – I was certain!'

'At the same time, there's nothing about violence on his record.'

Gently dug in his heels and went skidding down through the loose sand. At the moment he hadn't got time for Mixer. A little higher up the beach he could see the boats and the fishermen, and above them, on the hill, somebody painting at an easel. Two days ago hadn't she looked on this same scene?

At this point the shore was very slightly convex, but one could see at least a mile of beach in either direction. At quarter-mile intervals pillboxes had been built, a few of which remained poised drunkenly above the beach. On the nearest one of these some youths were performing acrobatics.

'What sort of fish do they catch?'

In the shallows a child with tucked-up skirt was pushing a shrimp net and looking the picture of earnestness. 'Soles ... plaice ... I don't know.'

Another, a little boy, was trying his best to fly a kite.

They came up with the boats, still a centre of interest. The reporter and his colleague were in conversation with the fishermen. One of the latter was showing the photographer where the body had lain; another, a freckled-faced youngster, was sweating over an engine.

'Any statement for us yet?'

'It was probably a man who did it.'

'You told us that before.'

'It could have been a woman.'

The reporter touched his photographer's shoulder. It wasn't often that one got a present like this! Gently, apparently unconscious of his picturesque qualities, continued his unhurried survey of the group of boats.

Of the seven, six were gaily painted and one alone was white. This was the boat in which the freckled youth was working at the engine. They were bluff-bowed, deep-bodied, powerfully built little craft, not more than seventeen feet long but big and burly for their size. Each had an 'S.H.' registration board bolted to its gunwale and its name, with suitable flourishes, carved in its transom. There was the *Girl Betty,* the *Boy Cyril,* the *We're Here,* and the *Willing*

45

Boys. The white boat had a varnished name board and was called the *Keep Going*.

Gently paused beside the latter, so utterly different was it from the others. Quite apart from the paint and the name board, it stood out as a separate species. It had a finish like a yacht. All the fittings were chromium plated. The paintwork had been built up until the surface resembled velvet, while the gunwale and the transom were of varnished teak that shone like glass.

'Is this one a pleasure boat?'

The youngster wiped his brow with a hand which left a greasy mark.

'There isn't a lot of pleasure in her!'

'No ... but does she go fishing?'

'W'yes, that's what she's for.'

'Then what was the idea of getting her up like this?'

'You'd better ask Mr Dawes – it just happen he take a pride in his boat.'

A wave of a spanner indicated the net store on the hill. Beside it was standing a tall fisherman with a white beard. He was leaning against one of the tarred posts from which the drying nets were slung; his eyes, staring out to sea, had the peculiar vacancy of seafaring men ashore.

'He like to show off his money!'

One of the fishermen spat contemptuously – the same man who had been showing the site of the tragedy to the photographer. He was a lean but powerfully built fellow of sixty or so. His face had a vindictive cast and his dark eyes looked angry.

'Boats like mine aren't good enough for Esau Dawes – did you ever see such truck on a longshore fishing boat? Next thing you know it'll be gold-plated ringbolts!'

'Shut you up, Bob!' came from several of his mates.

'Why should I shut up? I don't owe no-body no money!'

Gently hunched his shoulders and wandered over towards the gap. The *Keep Going*'s owner paid him no attention as he passed by. Fifty yards further on sat the young artist with his easel; he held a brush between his teeth while he stroked vigorously with another. An old umbrella tied to a broom handle was keeping the glare of the sun from his work.

'That's Simmonds ... you remember?'

If he did, Gently made no reply. Like any other curious stroller he went up to see what was happening to the canvas. Simmonds, a taut-faced young man with reddish-gold hair, charged his brush nervously as he felt himself being overlooked. He was painting a beachscape in rather sombre colours; he had perhaps noticed it and was now darkening his sky.

'Do you sell any of your pictures?'

Simmonds looked round quickly, flushing. He possessed wide hazel eyes which had an oddly vulnerable appearance. His lips made a perfect Cupid's bow and the lower one trembled.

'As a matter of fact I do!'

He was forcing a hardness into his voice.

'I've sold several pictures – I'm not entirely an amateur! Now; if you don't mind, I prefer not to talk while I'm working.'

'I thought I might buy one.'

Simmonds seemed more upset than ever. He attacked his sky with an awkwardness that threatened to ruin everything. In the background his tent looked snug with its flaps neatly rolled and tied. One of the tracks which intersected the marrams passed close beside it on the way from the village.

'What do you know about him?'

Dyson was eager to supply information. It was the first time since they had left the guest house that Gently had shown the slightest curiosity.

'His age is twenty-two. He comes from

48

Cheapham but he's living in Norchester. His mother is dead and he had a row with his father, who keeps a butcher's shop in Cheapham. He works for an insurance firm in Norchester, but his head is full of this artistic nonsense.'

'Who saw him with Rachel Campion?'

'A girl from the guest house, name of Longman.'

'What did she say they were doing?'

'Just walking on the beach. Simmonds was carrying his painting gear.'

'He's got good looks, of course.'

'Do you think – shall we pull him in?'

Gently smiled through his sweat.

'Let him finish his picture! We'll go back to the Bel-Air and have a long iced shandy.'

As Dyson said later, Gently had a genius for getting backs up.

CHAPTER THREE

The Bel-Air had an unsuspected merit: it really did seem cooler inside it than out. This may have been due to the trees, which were the only ones in Hiverton – they were wind-sculptured oaks and threw little enough shade, but their dark leaves tempered the all-pervading glare.

In the bar Maurice was serving milkshakes to a group of noisy teenagers. He seemed very popular with them and they all addressed him by his Christian name.

'Some of that pineapple, Maurice.'

'Maurice, make mine with maple syrup!'

A slim girl with a gamine cut had plugged in an electrical recorder. In a moment half of them were clapping and tapping to a recording of 'Jailhouse Rock'.

'How's our crime coming along, Maurice?'

'Jimmy looks like a killer, and he had a pash on her!'

'Is it right that there's a couple of Yard men down here?'

'Dig that boss of hers – he's got something on his conscience!'

Dyson had gone off to catch a bus into Norchester. He had got fed up with trying to help Gently. The manager of the Bel-Air, who wore a lounge suit despite the weather, had taken Gently aside for no conceivable reason. In his office he had produced a file of testimonials. One was signed by a former minister and another by a well-known comedian.

'This has always been a place with a reputation. I don't know how–'

'Nobody remembers what they read in the
papers.'

'I only hope we shan't have a rush of
cancelled bookings.'

He treated Gently to a drink and seemed
to want to hang on to him. Eventually he
was called away to conduct a telephone
conversation with some caterers.

Gently took his drink on to the lawn,
where he found a vacant deckchair. A maid,
not Rosie, was collecting glasses, and several
guests had woken up to give her fresh
orders. Mixer came by from the beach; he
clenched his hands and stared at Gently.
The tennis players, who had been sprawling
on the grass, suddenly all chased indoors to
fetch their swimsuits and towels.

'They tell me in the office...'

Gently was almost in a doze. The dead
woman's image was hypnotizing him, he
wanted to do nothing but puzzle and brood
over it. In his mind he had been fitting to it
one alternative after another.

'They tell me you're the bloke sent down
to take charge here.'

He opened his eyes, frowning, and found
that Mixer had come back. The man was

still clad in his trunks but with the addition now of a flowered beach shirt. The shirt was unbuttoned to reveal a hairy chest: Mixer was tanned all over, though some of it was probably stain.

'Aren't you Chief Inspector Gently?'

'What was it you wanted?'

'I want to have a talk – don't say you don't know who I am!'

Gently nodded indifferently. Several pairs of eyes were watching them. Mixer was using a blustering tone as though to challenge everybody's attention.

'I've got a right to have a word with you – this is a serious matter for me! Already people have got the idea...'

'You made your statement, didn't you?'

'Yes, but that's different.'

'You mean you want to add something to it?'

'It isn't that either. You know what I mean.'

Gently grunted. Yes, he knew! In his brief-case he had brought with him the thing that was worrying Mixer. It was headed 'Mixer, Alfred Joseph (*alias* Thomas Beaumont)'. It had been typed out for him by Records less than twelve hours before.

'Put yourself in my position. When it comes to a thing like this.'

The perspiration was trickling down through the hair on Mixer's chest.

'Now I want to get things straight. There's nothing I have to hide. Otherwise I'd have had my solicitor down – as yet I haven't bothered him.'

Not many of them were sleeping now, or even pretending to. The maid had come up with a fresh tray of drinks but her customers had mostly forgotten their orders.

'You want to talk about it here?'

Mixer dashed a furious glance at the audience.

'I don't see why I shouldn't, when everyone's so concerned! Right from the start they've picked on Alfie – that Inspector Dyson, too! Do you think they'd have called you in if there'd been half a case against me?'

'Let's go into the house.'

Gently rose from his deckchair. Mixer was sweating so much that his whole body seemed to run with it. Behind them, as they crossed the lawn, they heard a faint stir and murmur. Mixer clenched his fists convulsively and breathed heavily through his nostrils.

'Where is what they call the reading room?'

'This way – I shan't forget it in a hurry.'

'Suppose we get a drink?'

'Blimey, I could stand a dozen.'

In the bar the girl with her recorder was playing a treacly love song. Maurice was leaning across the counter and they were gazing into each other's eyes. The rest of the teenagers it seemed, had gone off somewhere.

'So I've been inside! Does it make me a crook?'

Mixer had a whining note in his voice which grated with Gently. The reading room was a gloomy place but not unsuited for interrogation. An architectural accident, it was remote from the rest of the ground-floor rooms; one reached it by a passage leading off near the main entrance.

'I made my mistake and I paid for it, didn't I? Since then I've gone straight, and nobody can say different.'

There were two mahogany bookcases and a varnished one with glass doors. The single window faced north and the atmosphere, strangely, had a schoolroom smell.

'All the same, you know how it is – once you've got a record you might as well hang yourself! That's why I kept quiet about it when big teeth was asking questions. Just let him get on to that, I thought, and I'll be inside before you can say "knife".'

'You must have realized.'

'That he'd get on to you blokes? That's just why I kept my trap shut – you and me talk the same language!'

Mixer pulled out his handkerchief and patted himself down with it. Gently had never seen a man in such a muckwash before. The fellow's skin was coarse and granular and he had tattoo marks on both wrists; his eyes, besides being small, were set so close that they gave a malformed appearance.

Yet this was the man whom Rachel Campion...

'Are you sticking to your story that she was just your secretary?'

'How do you mean – story? I'd like to see you prove different!'

'She was living at your flat, wasn't she?'

'I don't care if she was. I'm in business, see? I need a secretary. If they're not around all the time what good are they to you?'

'Even when you're on holiday?'

'That's just when things crop up.'

'What sort of things crop up?'

'Never mind – I wanted her around!'

Was it possible that he wasn't lying? Gently took a long pull at his clouded glass. When they had come in the window had been closed and still the air seemed completely stationary. Beyond the window was a view which included some of the council houses.

'Tell me something about her.'

'Eh? What do you want to know?'

'You've been living with her for a couple of years. You ought to know what she was like.'

Mixer looked puzzled.

'You've had a peek, haven't you? She was a classy bit of stuff, a proper lush girlie. She had all the charlies falling over their feet – not that they ever got anything out of her! And if you ask me–'

'Didn't she have a boyfriend?'

'Boyfriend?'

'She wasn't exactly a virgin.'

Mixer began dabbing again with his unfortunate handkerchief. As fast as he mopped it away the sweat came beading out afresh.

'How should I know? Perhaps she did – I didn't follow her about the whole time.'

'You were living in the same flat.'

'That's not to say I kept an eye on her.'

'You would know if anyone slept there with her, or if she stayed out at night.'

'She had her own key, that's all I can say. You can think what you like about the rest.'

'I think that she was your mistress.'

'And I say she wasn't! Can't a man have a pretty secretary without going to bed with her?'

Mixer seized his glass and gulped down about half the contents. He had a voracious way of drinking which made his small eyes bulge at each swallow. When at last he lowered the glass he exhaled his breath in a panting gasp.

Had Rachel Campion noticed it, or didn't she pay attention to such things?

'Where did you pick up with her?'

'She came through an agency.'

'We shall check up on that.'

'All right then – I met her at The Feathers in Oxford Street!'

'What do you know about her background?'

'I never knew she had any. She was living in rooms in Camden Town, and if she had any people she never mentioned them to me.'

'Hadn't she got some friends?'

'Only blokes running after her.'

'What about women?'

'She didn't get on with them.'

'Didn't she have any letters?'

'From blokes – she showed me some of them.'

'Can't you remember any names?'

57

'No – and she used to burn the letters.'

'Would you say she was an educated woman?'

'She was a Londoner like me. There wasn't nothing upshus about her, just one of the girls.'

A Londoner... Gently savoured the phrase, adding it to the picture he was striving to build. A Londoner like Mixer, a child of the grey streets. With a twang in her voice, a *savoir-faire*, a naïve gaiety: a native-born Londoner. And a proper lush girlie.

He moved over to the varnished bookcase and stared in at the unlikely contents. In the glass panel he could see Mixer clutching at his drink and throwing odd glances towards him. It was the bookcase, no doubt, which contributed that peculiar smell to the room.

'Was she hard up when you took her on?'

'Bits of stuff like that aren't never hard up.'

'How much did you pay her?'

'As much as she was worth.'

'Enough to give you the right to be jealous?'

'Who says I was jealous?'

'Everyone in the place – and also that you had a quarrel with her.'

This time Mixer didn't jump in with an immediate denial. Quite clearly, reflected by a set of *Harmsworth Encyclopedias*, a frown was making lines on his sloping forehead.

An ugly man! What in the world had she seen in him? With her attractions she might have had a handsome as well as a moneyed lover.

'Well then, suppose I did?'

He wasn't even clever. It had taken him thirty seconds to decide that this was his best answer, that it would give a little colour to his subsequent behaviour. Obviously, something had to explain his going off to Starmouth alone.

'What did you quarrel about?'

Again he was stumped for the quick answer.

'Which of them had gone to bed with her?'

'It wasn't like that! It was some letters.'

'Letters? What letters?'

'Some I wanted her to type.'

'How did that bring a quarrel about?'

'She – she wanted to go to that film show in Hamby.'

'But she didn't, did she?'

'How should I know what she did?'

'And she didn't type the letters – nor did you stay to dictate them to her.'

'It led to words, I tell you. I just got the car out and scarpered.'

Perhaps it wasn't such a bad story, considering the heat. Worse ones, told with conviction, had been known to influence juries. The fact it was a string of lies wasn't terribly important.

'So you took the car into Starmouth.'

Of this he had tended proof. It had consisted of a half ticket to a show running at the Albion Pier.

'That's right. I drove straight there. You can do any check-up you like. Got in there about half-six, I did, and went and had a drink at the Majestic on the front.'

'What did you do after that?'

'I booked my seat for Frankie Howerd. The girl there will remember me – tell her the saucy bloke what gave her a tip. Then I strolled up the front and looked at the girls. There was a blonde bit I took into the Bodega for a drink. After the show I had a snack in one of those caffs up Regent Road, then I picked up another bint and we did some snogging in the car.

'I got back here after twelve – ask Maurice, he saw me come in. I went straight up to bed and slept through till nine o'clock. I didn't know nothing about this lark until the maid brought in my breakfast. There isn't nothing against me – except the fact that I once did a stretch!'

It all came out with a rush, using practically the same words as appeared in his statement. The impression was that here Mixer was sure of his ground, that these were hard facts which would bear investigation. But why, in that case, was he frowning and sweating so much?

Did he know that Rachel might have been alive at one a.m.?

'These two women you mention – did they tell you their names?'

'The blondie did. It was Marilyn Lane. She was staying at the Gwalia in Dickson Road.'

'How about the other one?'

'I don't know about her. She was lit up – we both were – but not so as I couldn't drive!'

'And the name of the café?'

'I don't know that neither. There's a score of them at least up Regent Road.'

'Where did you park your car?'

'For the snogging? ... I drove a bit. It might have been Church Plain or somewhere round there. I was going to drive her home but she said she'd rather walk ... got something else in mind, I dare say!'

Yes, it was quite a good story as far as it went. Gently finished his shandy and set the glass on the reading-table. Mixer was watching him anxiously, handkerchief in hand. For

61

a wide boy with a good tale shouldn't he be worrying a little less?

'So we can't check your movements after eight-thirty that evening?'

'Eh?'

One could nearly see the sweat begin to break out in fresh rivulets.

'That was the time when the second house started at the Albion. After that we've got nothing but your word for it, have we?'

'But haven't I just said–!'

'You've said nothing that can be proved.'

'That woman – you can find her up.'

'In Starmouth? Without a name?'

The sweat was running down into Mixer's eyes. He had to keep dashing at it with the back of a hairy hand. His beach shirt, fresh on half-an-hour ago, was streaky and patched with dark areas of moisture.

'You can't prove it's not the truth.'

He made it sound like a question.

'You're picking on me, too – I've been inside, and that's all that matters!'

Gently shrugged his shoulders massively and found a seat on the table.

'Just listen to what I say, and don't bother to interrupt. This is the way Inspector Dyson sees it, and personally I don't blame him!

'Rachel Campion was your mistress and

you were as jealous as sin of her. She only stuck you for your money and she was unfaithful behind your back.

'At Hiverton she picked up with someone – never mind who it was. She was clever at concealing such things, and his identity doesn't matter. But the knowledge that she had a lover was eating into you like poison: you followed her, watched her, kept an eye on everyone, and on Tuesday you had a row about it and pretended to go off in a pique.

'In reality you were following a plan, and the first part of it was an alibi. For this you went into Starmouth and built up the story you've since told. Then you returned to spy on Rachel. You intended to catch her in the act. You had made up your mind to murder her if you found her with her lover.

'You did catch her and you strangled her. You were going to put the body in the sea. But then, when you got it to the beach, you found the fishermen there with their boats, and later on, when you returned, the tide was flooding and you couldn't put her in. So you left her on the beach. It was the only thing you could do. And you crept back to your bedroom, ready to be surprised at nine.

'Only – and this is the curious point – your Starmouth alibi doesn't cover you. She may have been dead when you say you got back, but on the other hand you still had time in which to do the job. Either way it's a fair case, and we might make it stick.

'Do you still think we're being unreasonable in viewing you as a suspect?'

Gently had rarely seen a human being reduced to such a mess. Mixer's streaming face was grey, his eyes staring like a sick dog's. His whole aspect, in fact, suggested that of a distempered animal. He breathed quickly and fiercely through dilated nostrils.

'On the other hand there's this in your favour.'

It was a toss-up whether Mixer was listening or not.

'You've given this alibi in apparent good faith, which suggests that you didn't know when Rachel Campion was killed. That doesn't let you out – it might simply mean that you're being clever! But on the whole, it would have been easier for you to have squared it than not. Only another thing hangs to it. For what, then, was the alibi? There's an odd smell about that, and I should like to know what it is.'

Mixer tried to wet his lips but they and his tongue seemed equally parched. His eyes had an unhinged expression as though he were losing touch with his surroundings.

'When did you say?'

He had to swallow several times.

'When did you say it happened?'

'I didn't, but it was some time between eleven and one.'

'Then!'

Colour rushed back. The eyes appeared to switch on.

'What were you going to say?'

'Nothing – only it wasn't me!'

A bell rang somewhere, perhaps the tea bell in the lounge. It was followed by a voice calling from one of the upper windows. Two youngsters ran up the path and disappeared into the hall: one heard the double clang of feet as they bounded over the door grille.

'I think you'd better listen to this.'

Gently was stung by the mistake he'd made. Mixer was dabbing his face again and flapping his shirt-front to cool himself. A moment ago he'd been putty, but now, inexplicably...

'You did two years for embezzlement – that's on the official record. But just in case you think we're asleep, here's the other part of the story.

'We know what your business is – you're a promoter of fake companies. Up till now you've been lucky with it, but don't let it kid you. And there's something else that interests us. A little matter of warehouse robberies! There've been six of them in the last two years from which connections have been traced to a certain Alfie Mixer.

'To be blunt, your career is just about to catch up with you, and this time it won't stop at a paltry couple of years. So if you know anything about this business you'd better spit it out – it might be worth a few summers spent in Pentonville or Wandsworth.'

He had struck the right note. Mixer's craven look returned. Twice he had tried to get a word in and now, when he did, his voice came in a sorry croak:

'You can't prove nothing about that!'

But the words lacked conviction – you could read his mind at a glance; as though his thoughts were being written across that sloping, sweating forehead.

'Have you nothing else to say?'

'I'm going to ring up my solicitor.'

'You'd do better to come clean.'

'I ain't done nothing. I'm going to ring him!'

People were coming in to tea and one could hear their muffled voices. A man laughed, a woman responded, perhaps with a touch of reproof in her tone. In the background a chink of cups had a cooling, relaxing sound.

'Get out then – I've finished with you!'

He felt a sudden surge of disgust with Mixer. A sweating, fearful lump of humanity – a criminal type, if such a thing existed! – and ugly: he was abominably ugly. What could it have been ... with a woman like Rachel?

When the man had gone he sat a long time musing, then, for no reason, went over to the window. The reading room faced north and the building's shadow lay that way. A deckchair was placed in it and in the deckchair sat Maurice. He turned to grin at Gently from a racing paper he was reading.

'After tea I've got a job for you.'

Dutt, as always, never obtruded himself. Now he was sitting on the verandah and patiently awaiting his senior's direction. After a dozen cases with Gently he knew roughly what was required of him.

'You're to take the car into Starmouth and to check on Mixer's alibi. Get in touch with Inspector Copping and show him a copy of the statement. While you're having tea I'll make a note or two in the margin.'

Dutt jerked his chin impassively; he, too,

was down to his braces and shirtsleeves.

'Think there might be something there, sir?'

'I'm not sure, Dutt. And I'd like to be.'

'I've been having a word with the kids, sir, and it all seems to hang together. It was a joke with them how jealous he was, and once or twice they saw him come out of her room. Trust youngsters to notice a thing like that.'

On the phone he talked to Pagram, his colleague at the Yard.

'What's it been like today?'

'Bloody awful! You're well out of it.'

'It couldn't be hotter.'

'You listen to this. We fried some eggs and bacon on a paving stone in the courtyard. Johnson had them for lunch and his picture's in all the evening papers.'

'I want some digging done.'

'You would, wouldn't you?'

'It's this woman who was strangled. I want to know who she was. Her last address before she went to West Hampstead was a furnished room in Camden Town.'

'Have you got the address?'

Gently thumbed open a sheet of note-paper. It was scribbled across in Mixer's primitive handwriting.

'Eighty-two Dalhousie Gardens. She left in

June a couple of years ago. No next of kin and no known acquaintances. Lower middle-class cockney – could be a native there.'

'What exactly are you after?'

'Every single thing you can get.'

Against the instrument Gently had propped his photograph. Its eyes, which had faced the camera, followed him about as he talked to Pagram.

CHAPTER FOUR

Dutt departed in the Wolseley, which Dyson had left at their disposal, and Gently had tea and toast in a corner of the lounge. Almost automatically he passed the guests under review; they fell, he noticed, into roughly two classes.

There were the youngsters, most of whom seemed to be on their own. Their ages appeared to range from about sixteen to twenty. Then there were the elderly people, some, no doubt, retired: a few of them, like Colonel Morris, were residents at the Bel-Air.

In between there was very little, and only one couple had young children. They were a pair from Wolverhampton and spoke with a broad Midland accent. Gently set down the husband as being a factory foreman or minor works official.

The teenagers were very conservative and wore almost identical clothing. It consisted of jeans and printed shirts, worn indiscriminately by both the sexes. The young men had crew cuts and the girls the gamine or urchin. They were a noisy crowd but strangely polite. They came, it seemed, from prosperous middle-class homes.

The older people were a very mixed bunch. They ranged from Colonel Morris, with his roguish eye, to a pair of severe old maids who were probably schoolteachers. One of them was a clergyman who loved to brandish obsolete words. Another, from his conversation, had trained racehorses in the north of England.

But they had this in common: they were civil and well bred. Even the Wolverhampton couple were on their mettle and determinedly fitting in. It was Mixer who didn't fit, who stuck out like a bunch of garlic. From their attitude it was clear that he'd been cold-shouldered from the first.

Gently watched him now, new-towelled and dressed, eating teacakes at his table.

70

Those who were nearest had their heads turned and the rest were refusing to see him. Sometimes a teenager threw him a quick look, then muttered a few words which provoked a giggle. Rosie and the other waitress attended to him with disdain: one could hear him eating the teacakes from the other side of the lounge.

A complete outsider! Couldn't even he feel it? Mustn't it have been the same when Rachel Campion sat opposite him ... except that, one and all, the male guests had been making eyes at her?

Even the conversation ignored him. It was running on anything but the tragedy. As though they had conspired to turn their mental backs as well, they deftly avoided referring to the subject. It was nothing to do with them they weren't people of that sort! By accident, perhaps, or managerial error.

Why did Mixer come here in the first place, or was it just that he didn't care?

Gently watched them leaving the lounge, one after another; first the teenagers in a body and then the others at intervals. Mixer was among the last to go. He had a surprising appetite for teacakes. Colonel Morris, thinking he was unobserved, pinched Rosie's behind and made her squeak.

'You're a wench-and-a-half, m' dear!'

'I've told you before, Colonel!'

Seeing Gently sitting in the corner the Colonel gave him the broadest of winks and strode out of the lounge as though he found the heat invigorating. Under his plate, Gently saw, he had left a florin for Rosie.

Outside the sun had slanted but things were really no cooler. Instead a subtle change had occurred in the atmosphere. The heat now seemed to float one, it derived equally from sun and ground; in place of the steady beating one was immersed in a bath of heat.

In going down to the beach Gently had no settled intentions. He had already funked several avenues at which Dyson had fumbled hopefully. So far, he had ignored the bridge players, who might have remembered something. And Maurice, who had seen her last … he had completely neglected Maurice!

To be honest, his approach was the reverse of businesslike. As usual he was following his instinct, or rather an innate feeling. Or, to be more precise, the ghost of Rachel Campion – she had got under his skin, that woman: still he couldn't exactly place her. She was fascinating him in death as she had done others during her lifetime.

Because ... what was it that had struck him, as he sat there munching his toast? Something important though half-recognized, a tiny spurt of revelation. It was that, unlike Alfie Mixer, Rachel had fitted in at Hiverton. Morals, cockney accent, and all, she had not been out of place.

But that wasn't so much to strain over, as though he were digging for a diamond! By all accounts she had behaved herself and been otherwise acceptable. Why then did it seem important and even curiously significant? It told him absolutely nothing except that Mixer might have underrated her background.

Had she been there before? That seemed improbable. A woman of her outstanding appearance would hardly have been forgotten. She was a stranger to the manager and also to the village: everyone had been intrigued but nobody had recognized her.

He strolled over to the boats, from which most of the fishermen had gone to tea. There remained only the *Keep Going*'s owner watching his young mechanic at the engine.

'Police. I'd like to ask you some questions.'

Both turned to look at him expressionlessly.

'It's about this woman who was killed. Had you seen her here before?'

They were a fair cross-section of witness, standing there, and shaking their heads. The boat owner was three score, the freckled youngster two-and-twenty. As soon as his question was answered they returned their attention to the engine.

No, it didn't lie there, the meaning he was trying to fathom. It was nothing so simple, nothing so easy to come at. Perhaps it would appear in Pagram's report, perhaps it would remain locked up in that photograph.

He turned his back on the boats and, plodding through sand and shingle, came to the firm wet level of the tideline. There were plenty of people about, more than had been there earlier. It was half-day closing in Norchester and Starmouth and his arrival, most likely, had been splashed over the lunchtime papers.

'Can't you give us something to go to press with?'

The first reporter had been joined by colleagues: now there were six of them, advancing on him almost menacingly. Two of the newcomers were carrying cameras. They wasted no time in committing his shirt and hat to celluloid.

'All right – you can print this.'

Notebooks appeared like lightning.

'As a result of our investigations enquiry has been extended to Starmouth and London. The dead woman is presumed to be a native of the London area and enquiries are being prosecuted at Camden Town.

'The police are eager to interview any person who was acquainted with Miss Campion. They are asked to get in touch with Chief Inspector Pagram, Central Office, New Scotland Yard (Whitehall 1212), or with their local police station.'

'You think someone followed her up here?'

Gently made an indefinite gesture.

'We've no positive reason for thinking so.'

'What are you looking for at Camden Town, then?'

How could he tell them what he didn't know himself?

After a little more prying they hurried off to phone their papers. A curious group had been attracted by the interview and Gently, irritated, went striding off along the tideline.

He didn't know himself – that was the worst of it! Without a single logical reason he was letting her personality dominate him. And there was no need to look abroad for people to suspect, when anyone who'd fallen heavily ... anyone with a latent streak... Mixer had a motive, but he wasn't alone in that.

A quarrel after they'd made love, followed by the shock of the limp-fallen body – anger, perhaps, because she had died so treacherously. And indignation with the fear as he tried to cover the deed. A crime he hadn't meant! A penalty that couldn't be just!

Why be complicated and subtle with facts which told their own story?

He kicked at the pebbles which came in his way. If only he could start again and begin to see things clearer. Yet could there have been another way except the one he was pursuing? Were the facts so very simple, when they began with Rachel Campion?

After walking till the sweat poured down he turned off into the sandhills. Here one imagined there would be a breeze, but in effect there wasn't a breath of one. The view, however, was extensive. Inland one could see a broad. To the north the sandhills stretched away to a soaring mound that marked the Ness, and southward, past the sprawl on the beach, to a bluish haze which was probably Starmouth.

He lit his pipe and looked around him. It was a lonely spot with a spirit of wildness. A lot of beach and a lot of marrams ... why did everyone cluster within a stone's-throw of the gap?

Between the line of hills and the first scant pasture would be two or three hundred yards of marram. It consisted of mounds and holes and ridges and was colonized by the grass and a few sea-favouring plants. Rabbits there would be, there, natterjacks, lizards. From time to time a bare foot would step on an adder. But there was no shade at all. No shade for miles. The sun roared down on the marrams like a celestial blowtorch.

He shook his head and set off again, for the village. He had come further than he intended, in his walk along the tideline. Ahead of him, in an endless series, stretched the summits of the sandhills, their tawny flanks soft and hot, their grass rough and spiteful. Who ever came that way unless it was Nockolds, the poacher?

As he blundered among the last of them he smelt an unexpected savoury odour: someone was frying sausages – out there, on the marrams! But the mystery was quickly solved. He had stumbled on to Simmonds's encampment. Over a spirit-stove set between beach cobbles the artist was cooking his evening meal.

'You've got a nice little spot here.'

Gently fanned his face with his hat. Simmonds, after a quick look at him, continued poking and turning his sausages. The compliment was not unmerited. The camp site really was well chosen. A flat-bottomed depression on the top of a hill, it almost hid the tent without at all obstructing the view. Also it was handy for the village, though still remote from the chilly hurly-burly.

'This isn't my first camp.'

There was a touch of pride in the young man's voice.

'I spend all my holidays this way. Last year I was painting in the Snowdonia area.'

'Alone, are you, always?'

'An artist doesn't want company.'

'What does your girlfriend say about it?'

'I don't happen to have a girlfriend.'

Gently looked round for a seat and chose a baulk of sun-whitened driftwood. While Simmonds was talking he had lit a second stove and placed a billy of water over it. Now he forked the sausages on to a plate and added boiled potatoes from a smaller billy.

'You've come to ask me some more questions, have you?'

His movements were self-conscious but he was well in control of himself.

'If it isn't too hot!'

'That's something I'm used to.'

'I wish I could say the same.'

'It's a matter of training oneself'

Gently nodded and smoked silently, letting the artist get down to his meal. On the beach below he could see some of the Bel-Air youngsters, three of them in the water and the rest tossing a ball about. Simmonds sat cross-legged before the taped-up flaps of his tent. He ate with a deft fastidiousness, sprinkling salt from a little tin.

'I only spoke to her twice, you know.'

'You've the advantage of me. I didn't speak to her at all.'

'You don't mind me going ahead with my tea?'

'Good heavens no. I had mine at four.'

The tent, the stoves, the utensils, the site, they all bore witness of tidiness and method. Within the tent one could see a pile of precisely folded blankets. Against the inner pole stood the canvas at which Simmonds had been working that afternoon.

'Among other things, there's the view from here.'

It was something which hadn't escaped Gently's notice. You could see the village, the beach, the marrams, and part of the track leading inland from the gap. The boats, however, were not included. They were obscured by the line of the hills and by the net store.

'That's Hazey Mere, away at the back there. You can make out the sails of the yachts on most days. Beyond the Ness is Sea Weston lighthouse, this way the water tower at Castra. And when there's rain coming up you can see Starmouth quite plainly – in fact, for subjects, I need only turn the easel round.'

'It sounds an ideal pitch.'

'I found it two years ago.'

'You've camped here before, then?'

'Only once, over a bank holiday.'

'When did you first meet Rachel Campion?'

'Last week. It's in the statement I signed.'

Gently knocked out his pipe, grinding the ashes under his sandal. Simmonds had finished his sausages and was emptying tinned rice on to a fresh plate. Beyond the bathers, but inshore, chugged a smart motor sailer. Further off was a white-painted vessel with a yellow funnel.

'Tell me exactly how you met her.'

'She came and watched me – while I was painting.'

'Here, do you mean?'

'No, higher up the marrams. I was painting the Ness and that great big sandhill.'

'What did she say?'

'I'm sorry, I don't remember. It was one of the silly things that people always think are clever.'

'And then?'

'She sat down and watched me. I don't like people doing that. In the end I simply packed up – it was nearly lunchtime, anyway.'

'And she came back with you?'

'Yes. As far as the gap. I had to go into the village to pick up some bread and some methylated.'

There was no doubt about his composure – or about the nervousness under it. It was a curious amalgam with an undertone of brittleness; he was like someone grasping a nettle or going deliberately to stand on a precipice. In a way it was touching, in a way it was droll. He was trying to be grown up while in fact he was still largely a boy.

'One thing I can tell you – she, wasn't just what they're making her out. She was intelligent, too. She knew something about art.'

'I thought she said something silly?'

'Yes, but that was just at first. Then she told me about a Braque exhibition she'd seen and asked if I liked Rouault. As a matter of interest, Rouault is one of my influences.'

'That was certainly intelligent of her.'

'She knew Dali, too.'

'I take it that you admired her.'

'Well ... I don't know about that!'

He finished the rice with a flush on his tight, well-drawn features. Then, the water having boiled, he measured in tea and removed the billy.

'Can I offer you a cup?'

'I think I could manage one.'

It was served in an aluminium mug which burned the lips, but had the strong fragrance of tea made in camp-fire fashion.

'No, she wasn't just ... one of those, if you understand my meaning. She was beautiful, I admit, but that's not the same. And she was friendly, too. She was easy to talk to. With women, as a rule ... she was different from other women.'

'When was the other time you spoke to her?'

'A day or two later. It was the same as the first time – she came to watch me painting. To be quite honest' – Simmonds hesitated awkwardly – 'I made a pencil sketch of her. I didn't tell that to the other man.'

He waited for Gently to say something, but when he didn't, rose uncertainly to his feet. Gently sat with unchanged expression though his whole being had been suddenly alerted. It was as though he had heard a word in a secret language, a mystic signal of significance.

'There ... but it isn't very good, I'm afraid.'

Simmonds had fetched a framed satchel from the tent. Keeping the flap between Gently and himself, he pulled out a sheet of rough-surfaced drawing paper. On it, at about half life-size, was a portrait head of Rachel.

'Actually, I'm better with a brush.'

'Here – hand it over to me.'

Gently grabbed the sheet impatiently and turned himself to shade it from the sun.

It was a rubbed atmospheric drawing; it differed surprisingly from the photograph. The face was the same, the features were rendered accurately, but the expression was quite other than that captured by the camera. A maternal expression ... was that possible? Apparently it was, if one could rely on Simmonds. The dark eyes were now tender, generous, beneficent. The lips, relieved of sensuality, had an unconscious little smile. Yet there was nothing idealistic in the manner of the drawing. If anything it was heavy, due to an uncertain technique. At twenty-two the artist was still fumbling for adequacy: whatever he had brought out had been achieved accidentally.

'Let me see the rest of them.'

'Rest of them ... do you mean?'

'This isn't the only one – you've got a whole bagful. Just hand it over, and I'll sort them out.'

Simmonds was reluctant but he made no objection. Like a well-brought-up child he handed Gently his satchel. Then he stood by, slightly flushed, his chestnut hair hanging over his forehead. Again he was like a child, one who had passed up a good essay.

'Excepting that one they're from memory.'

There were fourteen drawings, of a single subject.

'As you see, when it comes to paint...'

A canvas, depicting Rachel wearing only the lower half of a bikini.

'But don't think for a moment.'

'How long did it take you?'

'Take me?'

'To paint this. *It* wasn't done from memory!'

Gently planted the canvas carefully on the forks of the baulk of driftwood. Simmonds wasn't making a mistake when he supposed he was best at paint. Colour was clearly his *forte;* he could make it burn and scintillate. There were overtones of Gauguin in this Rachel among the marrams.

'It's done from life, isn't it?'

'Not necessarily.'

'It is! And not at one sitting – or lying, to be precise.'

'Suppose I were to say...'

'Just stick to the truth.'

'All right then, if you insist. I suppose I've got to tell you.'

But now he was shaking, for all his assumed composure. His coolness was too unnatural and he was appearing to notice it. Strangest of all, he had become apologetic, he seemed to want to please Gently, and as he talked he kept throwing the detective little ingratiating glances.

'It was she who suggested it, that first time we met. I did the first sketch I showed you, and she wanted me to do an oil. So then we arranged it. She came whenever she could. We went a good way up the marrams, of course, so that people wouldn't see her.'

'And naturally, you made love?'

'No! That's just what you mustn't think. Never once was there anything like that, even though she took her top off.'

'You simply got on with your painting.'

'Yes, that was the idea.'

Gently gazed at the eloquent canvas. Was it within the bounds of credibility? Had the little fool sat there, staring, painting, and never once gone over to try his luck with her? It wasn't a sisterly pose, that one of Rachel's. It could hardly have been made more provocative had she tried. One leg was crooked voluptuously, one lying straight, her breasts pouting skywards, her black hair sweeping the sand. And almost sliding from her hips the bare apology for a garment.

'How many times altogether?'

'Six, including the first.'

'Then why did you tell Inspector Dyson two?'

'She was murdered, wasn't she? I didn't want to get involved.'

Simmonds shivered, even as he tried to give one of his winsome looks. His hazel eyes followed Gently with spaniel-like eagerness.

'On what days did you meet her?'

'The first time was Monday ... that was last week. Then again on Wednesday and Thursday, Saturday, Monday...'

'And Tuesday – go on.'

Simmonds winced as though Gently had struck him.

'I know – I was going to say it! But it was only in the afternoon.'

'What time do you say she left you?'

'At – at half past four, I think.'

'The painting was finished. Why didn't

you give it to her?'

'It wasn't dry, and I wanted to touch it up.'

'And the rest of the day?'

'It's in my statement.'

'You mooned around the beach and went to bed sharp at eleven.'

Simmonds still struggled for a smile but the result was wry and tremulous. He wanted to please so much ... if only Gently would let him! There was nothing, his eyes seemed to say, which couldn't be explained and understood.

'Didn't you ever want to be her lover?'

Gently was turning over the various sketches. A few of them had the madonna-like look but none of them the fiery passion of the photograph.

'No it wasn't like that.'

'What was it like, then? You tell me.'

'She was simply a model.'

'Lay off it! I know better.'

'Well of course, if you mean...'

'Five days you were watching her. Five days she was lying there, naked, waiting. And you want me to believe...'

'It's true. You've got to!'

'But you wanted to, didn't you? It's only human nature. There were times when it was hard to keep your brush moving – times when you were only dabbing around on the palette. But you tell me there was nothing in it – what was up? Wouldn't she let you? Kept you sitting there looking and being a good boy?'

'But honestly, I tell you...'

'Pretended you were too young?'

'Believe me, you've got it wrong! It wasn't like that at all.'

Gently shrugged, shuffled the sketches and slipped them back into the satchel. Simmonds was all but wringing his hands in his efforts to convey his good faith.

'You've got to see – she was friendly. I haven't got a lot of friends! At home it was impossible. I did the only thing I could. Now, for over a year ... can't you see what I mean? Other people don't understand me ... she ... since my mother died...'

'You were fond of your mother, were you?'

'*She* understood me!'

'How old was she when she died?'

'People thought she was my sister.'

'And that's why these drawings?'

'...drawings?' He flushed hotly. 'It's not that – you can't get it straight! – though perhaps, in a way...'

'Still, it's interesting, isn't it?'

Gently slid in the canvas after the

sketches. For a moment, as he buckled the straps, his eye dwelt strangely on the artist. Below them now the Bel-Air youngsters were ragging and rolling in the sand; the motor sailer was out of sight, the Swedish vessel replaced by a tanker. The sun, at long last, was taking definite steps westward.

'I'll keep these for the moment – they'll be taken care of. In the morning I'll want a fresh statement. Is that understood?'

'If you like I'll write it out.'

'It won't be necessary. Just make certain there's nothing else that you forgot to tell Inspector Dyson.'

He left Simmonds standing helplessly with new expostulations on his lips. Coming towards them with an eager step he could see the reporter of the *Echo*. And by the net store, though well out of earshot, the owner of the *Keep Going* had his eye on them.

Except possibly up in the marrams, there was nowhere private at Hiverton.

CHAPTER FIVE

For a good hour past he had been wandering about the village, staring at everything and gaping at everybody: why, he would have been perplexed to answer. One hadn't to go far to see the whole of Hiverton. It was huddled together like a misplaced hill village. On one side was the sea, on the other stony fields. From a little distance it had the appearance of a watchful, red-brick citadel.

He had plodded along the terraces which formed the northerly ramparts, turning deliberately from one to another until he had covered every yard. Here jerrybuilding had flourished in the years between the wars. The houses were sullenly ugly, needed plaster, needed paint. They were served by unmade-up roads. The yards behind them were small and slummy. In front they had patches of scuffed grass or anaemic flower beds edged with bottles. The paths to them, almost without exception, were of trodden earth, cinder, and cockleshells.

And the people who lived in these places?

At the thought he had hunched his shoulders. Yet something about them had struck him, difficult though it was to put it into words. He had met them coming out, seen them trudging up to their doors; here one had passed a civil word, there one plucked a curtain to stare at him. But in total, what was the impression? It was escaping him, for the moment. Unconsciously, intuitively, he had made a judgement, which later would reappear in the guise of inspiration.

Now he was standing at the crossways, at the physical heart of the village. Three other shops besides the Beach Stores each faced the irregular plain. A butcher's – wasn't that the place where Simmonds had bought his sausages? – a baker's which dabbled in groceries, and a grocer who dabbled in bread. In fact, all the elements of a satisfying focal centre, helped out by the bus turnround, a chapel, and the post office. Then why did it fail, as if put together by an inept artist? Why did one's eye go perpetually roaming after a factor that wasn't there?

It was meaningless – that was the word! But one was checked directly by the paradox. There was plenty of meaning to be found in Hiverton, it was active and busy in its peculiar way. Only the word, once hit on, began to haunt Gently. It had an uncanny aptness which wouldn't let him alone. In some sense to be decided he knew it was applicable: to someone, somehow, Hiverton was devoid of meaning.

Still puzzling, he went up the steps to the Beach Store. Mrs Neal gave him a smile and a nod over her bacon slicer. By now, like everyone else, she would know his identity, and was probably expecting an official visit from him. Gently had read her statement, which confirmed that of Nockolds. There was plenty of routine that he had studiously neglected.

'Heard from your husband yet, Mrs Betts?'

A neat, drab woman stood waiting with a partly-filled rush bag.

'I had a letter from him this morning. They've done with the mackerel. They'll be working round this way for the season before long.'

'They're usually back at Starmouth by the first week in September ... let's hope it's a better herring-fishing this year than last.'

'The Scots boats are coming for all they said last time.'

Bacon, tea, and the latest gossip, and you could supplement the news with a copy of the local 'evening'. Gently picked one up from a pile on the stationery counter. It wasn't carrying his picture although his arrival had made the headline.

'My boy Tommy was telling me that the police are properly stumped.'

Mrs Neal hissed something in a whisper and her customer turned to stare at Gently.

'Well, I suppose one can speak!'

'That's five-and-seven, Mrs Betts.'

The drab woman stalked out offendedly with the air of a hen driven from its hopper.

Mrs Neal came round the back of the counters. She beamed at Gently as though it were a great joke. She had a twinkle of transparent malice in her eye: it was this that gave point to the plump good nature of her face.

'I suppose you get used to being gawked at and talked about? It's just a job, like everything else, though I wouldn't want it myself.'

'Aren't you in the same position?'

'Here, you mean, behind the counter?'

'I should have thought they talked about you.'

'Oh, they do! Don't you live in a village?'

Again that flash of unconscious malice, drawing a smile of response from Gently. He knew now what it was that attracted him to Mrs Neal. She was someone who understood Hiverton and understood it with detachment. More, unless he mistook her, she understood it with affection; he felt a twinge of surprise that such a thing was possible.

'Of course, when you came in here I didn't know you from Adam. It took half-an-hour for the word to get round. I've been wanting to have a talk with you. It's about Fred Nockolds. There's no harm in Fred, you know, but this business has got him worried.'

'About what he was doing there?'

'Yes ... exercising his dog!'

'It's a bit thin, isn't it?'

'Go on! He's up there regular.'

Gently brooded a moment, mentally reviewing Dyson's file. In effect he had long dismissed Nockolds from his thoughts. The poacher, who worked at a farm a mile outside the village, had been assisting in a calf delivery at the critical period. The vet and two witnesses had established this fact. 'I think we can accept his story.'

'He'll be relieved. Can I tell him?'

'You can if you like, but I'll be seeing him myself. By the way wouldn't he have had a gun and stuff on him?'

'There you are again! But he reported to Ferrety, didn't he?'

Her husband came in, a smooth-faced man with a bald patch. He related afresh how he had accompanied Nockolds to the beach. Gently listened, his eyes closed, trying to visualize the scene. Had the body then been there two hours, or was it only one?

'Did anyone get to the beach before you?'

'If so I didn't see them. But we couldn't shut the dog up and they soon started coming. It's a rum thing, that, how a body can upset a dog.'

'Did you notice any tracks?'

'It's all tracks unless there's been rain.'

'What about the fellow in the tent?'

'I didn't see him come down till later.'

'*He's* a queer one, if you like,' Mrs Neal interrupted them. 'Not that I think any ill of the lad, though there's nasty talk going round.'

'What sort of talk is that?'

'Why, that he's the one you're after. But I say it's all nonsense, and I see as much of him as anyone. There's nothing wrong there that a good home wouldn't put right.'

'You know about him, then?'

'Of course. He's often in for a chat.'

'Did he ever mention Miss Campion?'

'No. It's his mother I usually hear about.'

It was still hot enough for ice cream and Gently took a cornet out with him. From the steep-roofed buildings long shadows were falling, but a thermometer on the wall had only just sunk below eighty. One of the village children had got a bike and they were all having fun with it. As he raced across the open space they tried to catch him and pull him off. Two or three of the older ones sat apart on a bench. They glanced sideways at Gently, muttered furtively to each other.

He paused outside The Longshoreman, before which were parked several cars. The windows were open upstairs and down and one could hear the chatter of the bar from the road. Some young men, probably farm workers, sat drinking on two outside seats. They wore white shirts and their tanned flesh looked hard and healthy. Although they had only been talking cricket they, too, subdued their voices.

It was the same when he entered the bar: a lively scene seemed suddenly to hesitate. At the end of the room a game of darts was in progress and above the quick hush one could hear their soft thumping.

'Give me a glass of bitter.'

Without appearing to look round he was nevertheless taking it in. Fishermen, farm workers, one or two who worked in Starmouth: The Longshoreman was for regulars, people who fitted into their niche. On a trestle table under the window four old fishermen were shuffling dominoes. Round the dartboard they spoke in monosyllables and changed places automatically.

'Have this one on the house.'

But Gently tendered his coin firmly. The publican, stout and middle aged, gave him a solemn wink as he returned the change.

'*We* can't complain of the weather!'

He leaned confidentially on his massive elbows.

'If there's anything you want to know ... but I'd sooner it was in the back room. I try to please everyone. That's the tricky part of pub business.'

Gently grunted indefinitely and settled his hip against the bar.

The hush which marked his arrival had passed, though the conversation was perhaps quieter than before. One quickly became aware of different groups among the patrons. The fishermen, in particular, stuck very much together. The dart players were largely farm workers, those round the bar from town. In a corner by himself sat the *Keep Going's* owner; he smoked twist in a clay pipe, taking slow, measured puffs.

'That's Esau – Esau Dawes.'

The publican had followed his glance.

'You've seen his boat, haven't you? It's a hard one to miss! That's Jack Spanton, his mate, the young fellow having a joke. They think the world of that boat, it's like it was a human being to them.

'Then there's Josh Ives, the short 'un. Him and Aaron Wright are mates. They got blown up with a mine, which is where Josh got his limp from.'

'On the left it's Peero Palmer – you'll maybe hear them call him "Dutchy". Took his boat across to Holland, he did, and never came back till five years later.'

'Who's the one they're trying to shut up?'

'Him?' The publican looked uneasy. 'Don't pay any attention! It's Bob Hawks of the *Boy Cyril*. But he went queer years ago – which is saying something, when it comes to fishermen. They aren't ordinary people like you and me.'

It was the angry-eyed man whom Gently had seen talking to the reporters. Now, seemingly the worse for drink, he was angrier than ever. Every once in a while his voice would rise above the general hubbub, and his mates, who were soberer, could do nothing to stop him.

'There isn't a man among you...'

'Keep you quiet, Bob!'

'... not one, I say...'

'You've had too much into you.'

For a little while they could drown him but always he broke through again. His voice was hard and strident and full of uncertain accusation.

'He doesn't usually get drunk,' muttered the publican apologetically. 'He's too mean as a rule – he watches every penny. Some of them now ... look at Esau over there! He gets drunk every night and you can't tell him from sober.'

Gently finished his glass and the publican promptly refilled it. He was sticking to Gently as though to give him a personal sponsorship. From time to time he was summoned away to replenish other glasses, but always he hurried back to plant his elbows by the silent detective.

'There's always a lot said when a thing like this happens. A couple of pints – you know how it is! But they don't mean any harm by it, that's what I say. They come here to let off steam and to work it out of their systems.'

'Who's the mate on the *Boy Cyril*?'

'Abby Pike – that's him lighting his pipe. Another rum bloke! He's been married three times. During the war he went minesweeping and got a couple of bullets in him.'

Was it his imagination or had the atmosphere really become more tense? During the last few minutes, he thought, the various groups had shrunk further away from each other. Those clustered round the bar had got their backs turned to the rest; they were discussing a make of car with a conscious deliberation. At the dartboard there was silent attention, scarcely a word even being exchanged. And the fishermen had contracted their knot – only Dawes puffed on in oblivion.

'None of you seem to realize...'

The tipsy fisherman's voice rose again. His drinking had made it unsteady but the actual words came clearly enough.

'...one point of view, that's your whole trouble! One point of view ... no feeling at all...'

'Go and see to your nets, Bob.'

'It's the truth ... and you know it...'

'Can't you shut him up, Abby?'

'...you don't like to hear it!'

The publican juggled clumsily with a couple of tankards. Beer slopped into the drip pan and made a river along the bar.

'If ever there's anything to mob about here!'

He grabbed up a dishcloth to restore the situation.

Over at the trestle table they had finished their game of dominoes and one old gentleman was muttering to the others. Dawes's mate, Jack Spanton, had pulled out a mouth organ. He was playing it with a good deal more brio than feeling.

'...that girl, I say!'

Now Hawks was having to shout, and his eyes, dark and spiteful, were darting towards Gently.

'None of you cares a damn – laugh, it's all you can do! And what are they doing about it ... nothing ... stand there drinking beer!'

'What are you doing yourself, Bob?'

'...stand there, I say!'

There was a storm of nervous laughter during which Pike tugged at Hawks's sleeve. One or two of them, taking the cue, began singing raggedly with the mouth organ. The publican bawled for clean glasses, ignoring a trayful that stood under his nose.

'She meant a lot to somebody.'

The note had changed to one of pathos.

'Don't you ever think? That girl was someone's daughter, I tell you! How would you like it ... put yourself in his place. And her mother – think of that! Her mother ... didn't she have one too?'

His voice broke absurdly in alcoholic grief.

Tears ran down his thin cheeks, the corners of his mouth twitched downwards. Yet somehow he escaped being funny, this old man weeping into his beer. He was like a ham actor whose sham sentiments revealed a real tragedy. The long, bitter face seemed a picture traced by ancient suffering.

'...little sister ... brother perhaps. You aren't to know who she's left behind. And what do you care, any of you? Not a dashed thing! All you can think about ... isn't it the truth? She's dead ... lay there strangled ... and that's all you can think about!'

He drew a sleeve across his mouth and then gulped down some more beer. For a moment it looked as though the lachrymose vein would continue. But instead, he took a couple of belligerent steps towards the bar.

'And I ask you again ... what are they going to do about it? Where are these blessed policemen who ought to be on the job? Here's one ... just look at him. Holding up the bar! It isn't his daughter, so what does he care? Holding up the bar, and listening to every mortal word.'

It was useless singing any longer, Hawks had gone too far for that. Swaying slightly on his feet, he was menacing Gently with his empty tankard. Spanton's mouth organ clattered to the floor. The dart players ceased to throw their darts. Up and down the crowded bar there was a moment of bated, watchful silence.

And then, from Esau's corner, came the scrape of a table pushed aside. Sparing a glance from the threatening Hawks, Gently saw the big man get to his feet. There was nothing hurried about it. Esau's movements were slow and gentle. Taking all the time in the world, he settled a sea cap on his white head.

'Esau ... you let me be!'

Hawks's tone was suddenly apprehensive. He stumbled back a pace and let the tankard fall to his side.

'You haven't got no right. Esau, listen ... I'm warning you!'

Esau, deaf as the Ailsa Craig, continued his preparations for leaving. He shut his clasp-knife and put it away. He wrapped up his pigtail in a scrap of oilcloth. Pipe and matches went each into a stowage, and finally he drained what was left of his beer.

'I tell you, Esau!'

Esau patted his pockets.

'If you lay a hand on me!'

Esau took him by the arm.

There was no fuss about it and not another

word. Hawks, the wind quite out of his sails, was walked out like a child. Somebody grabbed the tankard from him, somebody else gave him his cap. The whole business was so quiet that one could scarcely believe it had happened.

'Phew!'

The publican made a gesture of wiping his brow.

'I thought there'd be trouble there, Esau or no Esau. That Hawks ... he's a wicked so-and-so, even when he's cold sober.'

'They'll be all right, will they?'

'Oh yes! You don't know Esau. You might say he's the skipper here – they all pay attention to him. And one time him and Hawks were mates on a drifter together.'

At first they wondered how Gently would take it, but he continued to lean, apparently unmoved, at the bar. Eventually Spanton rescued his mouth organ and the dart players cleaned their board. The publican, in a great bustle, filled a great many empty glasses.

If anything, the incident seemed to have cleared the air a little. The exclusive grouping of the company was beginning to relax. Gently, pipe between his teeth, listened amiably to the publican's chatter; one would have thought his only interest there lay in a pint in congenial company.

'Then, of course, you never saw her alive.'

Was it Hawks or was it Dawes whose departure had eased the tension?

'Not that she ever came in here, mind you.'

Or was it just that they'd weighed him up, deciding that probably he wasn't a trouble maker?

Spanton had succeeded in collecting a crowd round him. He'd got one of the ancients singing 'The North Sea Fisherman'. After that it was 'Stormy Weather, Boys', of which they all knew the chorus: Aaron Wright sang the verses, and it was the unexpurgated version.

Yes, the tension had relaxed – but wasn't it now, perhaps, too boisterous? From one extreme it had gone to the other, like a fit of malarial fever. Every moment it was growing noisier, more hectic, more reprehensible.

'How much is on the slate?'

'Come on, don't be awkward!'

'Just take it out of this, will you?'

'Well, if you say so.'

Had he missed something important by the skin of his teeth?

Outside the long twilight had commenced under a pale sky. Stars prickled overhead, and the coppery west suffused opalescence.

Round a shrub in someone's garden moths tapped and buzzed eagerly, while bats, scarcely audible, pipped as they flickered high above.

At the turn by the council houses he almost ran into a couple of lovers. They were leaning over a bicycle, heads together, very quiet. Then again, by a field gate, another silent couple. Their eyes followed Gently but they didn't draw apart.

On such a night as this ... two evenings ago. Hadn't the Bel-Air been nearly empty and Mixer, presumably, in Starmouth?

An alien fragrance reached his nostrils as he approached the gates of the Bel-Air. Dawes, another ghost of the twilight, sat solemnly smoking on a hedge bank.

'You wanted to see me, did you?'

The white head nodded very slightly. After an instant's hesitation Gently sat down on the bank beside him. It was a pleasant conference seat: the bank was tall with summer grasses.

'Bob Hawks ... I wouldn't pay much regard to him.'

The voice was like the man, slow, but full of grave decision.

'He's had his trouble, Bob has, and sometimes it makes him hasty. But I've had a word or two with him. I can answer that he'll watch his tongue.'

'What sort of trouble has he had?'

Dawes didn't appear to hear him. One had the impression that he was unused to being questioned, that wherever he found himself his word was the law. Having made his pronouncement, he sat a long time silent. The smoke proceeded from his mouth with a clock-like regularity.

'If that's all you've got to say...'

'Don't be in a hurry.'

He hadn't even looked at Gently, just sat there staring at nothing.

'You were talking to that boy.'

'Simmonds, you mean – the one with the tent?'

'I was wondering how much he told you.'

'Naturally, that's confidential.'

Another silence, this time more irritating. At the mention of Simmonds Gently's interest had been sharply roused. But he could see that it was useless to try hurrying the old autocrat. For years, very probably, Dawes had ruled the Hiverton roost.

'Did he tell you he got a thrashing?'

For answer Gently shrugged.

'So he didn't – I thought as much. They don't like to admit it, these youngsters.'

'Who gave him the thrashing – you?'

Dawes puffed impassively four or five times.

'Him up there who they say you've got an eye on.'

'Mixer – the man who was with her?'

'He found them together in the tent.'

Now there was room for a pause – Gently was frankly taken aback. So there had been more to the Simmonds story – apparently, a very great deal more! Simmonds had been leading him up the garden ... as a matter of fact, he had almost convinced him.

'How do you know about this?'

'Saw it happen. From the net store.'

'When?'

'Last Tuesday, just before tea.'

'Describe it to me.'

'That's all there is to it.'

'How long had they been in the tent – how did Mixer come to find them?'

Esau shifted his long legs as though to express his disapproval. Nobody badgered him like that, the slow movements seemed to say.

'I've seen him once or twice trying to find them up the marrams. Tuesday he hung around near the tent – have you seen that old pillbox? So then they came back and went

108

into the tent together. He ran across there like a madman and hauled the boy out by his ankles.'

'And the woman – what about her?'

'She came out of her own accord.'

'Didn't she try to intervene?'

'She might have said something, but that's all.'

'And when it was over?'

'Why, he marched her off with him. They came by the store and went off towards the guest house.'

'What were they saying as they passed you?'

'Nothing I heard. But they looked the more for it.'

'When was the next time you saw her?'

'Under the sacks by Bob Hawks's boat.'

'Who else saw it happen?'

'There wasn't only me.'

'Then why didn't you report it?'

'Didn't think to till I saw you with the boy.'

Esau scratched a leisurely match, his pipe having died on him. The bobbing flame lit his stern features with their viking-like cut. In his ears he wore gold rings, his beard was brushed to a point. His blue eyes seemed permanently fixed on some far-distant horizon.

But they saw plenty, those eyes, there was

no doubt about that.

'And what else do you know?'

'Nothing – about your business.'

'I shouldn't think you're one to miss much.'

'Nor one to talk about it, neither.'

'Perhaps I'd better remind you.'

But Gently could see it was a waste of time. The Sea-King of Hiverton had concluded his audience: there was nothing more to be got from him but steady puffs of smoke.

Still, he hadn't done so badly for his first day on the case. Gently got to his feet feeling that things had woken up a little. He'd got a handle now, both for Simmonds and for Mixer – especially on the latter he could put a little pressure!

Eager to press home his advantage, he nearly bowled over a hurrying Dutt. The sergeant was coming out of the Bel-Air and seemed in a state of high excitement.

'I've been back half-an-hour, sir!'

'What's the matter, Dutt – something popped?'

'Popped is right, sir – listen to this! It isn't quite what you might have expected.

'There's been a flap on at Starmouth – they've had some charlies raiding a warehouse. It took place on the Wednesday morning and there were four of them involved.

Now one of them meets the others at a caff on the Castra Road – his description fits our Mixer – and he was driving a green Citroen!

'That's all, sir, excepting they've got witnesses who can identify him. I told them we'd bring him back, and they're waiting for us now.'

CHAPTER SIX

It wasn't exactly a race into Starmouth, but it developed into something distinctly undignified. Gently, whose driving was usually unexceptional, was led into small but reprehensible excesses.

The lounge of the Bel-Air was where it had started. Mixer had installed himself there with whisky and a sporting paper. As soon as Gently entered he was set on by two reporters; one of them he had seen before, but the other was a fresh arrival.

'They'll just be in time to catch the early edition.'

'My editor's been in touch with the Yard.'

Like a couple of terriers they yapped round his heels, pushing, keen eyed, determined to get some copy from him. From his basket chair Mixer cast them apprehensive glances. Gently swore under his breath. This would have to happen!

'Come into the bar, will you?'

He appeared to capitulate, but on the way he had exchanged a couple of quick words with Dutt. Five minutes later he had heard the Wolseley's horn sound twice: at the first excuse he had terminated his impromptu press conference.

The trouble was that they had been too sharp for him, that pair of reporters. They had smelled a rat, they had shadowed Gently out of the house. Apparently it was their Morris which stood parked on the gravel, and the Wolseley had scarcely reached Hamby before headlights began to pursue it.

So he had stood on the accelerator, foolishly, needlessly. He had practised several little tricks to get rid of those persistent lights. At Castra he'd turned left and gone round the houses, and again at Starmouth he'd done his best to shake them off.

And all to no purpose – they had stuck to him like pitch. Getting a big kick, no doubt, out of chasing a police car. While all the time he'd known that he was being a trifle childish, that at the bottom of it he was upset by this

112

new and perplexing development.

'This sort of lets him out sir.'

Dutt had quickly put his finger on it. Yet it didn't let him out, not in a way that closed the file on him. Mixer, if it was he, had met his associates soon after midnight. In other words he could have strangled Rachel and still been in time to keep his rendezvous. But the probability had lessened, it had lessened considerably. With a robbery on his plate Mixer would hardly have chased back to Hiverton. Hadn't he already eased his feelings by giving Simmonds a pasting? Wouldn't he have lectured Rachel and perhaps threatened her with some punishment?

For this one night, at all events, he'd have let the matter ride. With three assistants down from town he couldn't afford to play the jealous lover.

To which one had to add his reactions when he heard the time of her death. One could read them clearly now – he knew he was safe from the capital charge! If the worst came to the worst, then he'd a cast-iron alibi! In his own mind he must have been confident that the warehouse job would clear him.

Yet ... that little doubt remained. He *could* have got back to murder Rachel. Even – though criminals were rarely so devious – he could have planned the robbery for insurance. He might have driven back to Hiverton with her murder expressly in his mind.

It was perplexing and unsatisfactory, an untidy bundle of facts. In sum it was getting one nowhere, it simply had the appearance of progress. Mixer had the better alibi – but he also had the better motive.

Gently dragged the Wolseley to a standstill before the steps of Starmouth Borough Police H.Q. Behind him he heard a squeal of tyres followed almost immediately by running feet. A photographer bounded on to the steps, his camera poking at the ready: he got a beautiful shot of Dutt shoving Mixer out on the pavement.

'That's Alfred Mixer, isn't it?'

'You'll get a statement later.'

'Is it an arrest or are you just detaining him?'

'Later, I said! Do you think we've nothing else to do?'

Mixer covered his face as he was hustled up the steps. He'd said scarcely a word on that journey into Starmouth. In the lobby they were met by Copping, with whom Gently had worked before. The Starmouth inspector shook hands cordially and signed to Dutt to take Mixer into a waiting-room.

'That's him, I'm willing to swear to it! We've got two independent descriptions. One is the watchman, who they left tied up, and the other the proprietor of the café where they met. Do you think that, now we've got him, we can get a line on the others?'

'If he's your man then you can rely on Records.'

Copping led him to the super's office where Symms himself was waiting for them. There was further handshaking and exchanges of compliments. The office, Gently noticed, had been redecorated. The last time he was there it had been a depressing blue.

'Your man gave you an outline?'

The super was his old spry self, spare, military, his small moustache crisply trimmed.

'I'd like to have some details – Mixer is suspect in the other business. I don't think there's much connection, but a check won't do any harm. And by the way ... if your canteen's open ... I managed to miss my supper.'

Copping dispatched a constable with an order of coffee and sandwiches. Gently reversed himself a chair and stuck his empty pipe in his mouth. From somewhere down the corridor came a murmur of voices – volunteers, he guessed, for the identity parade impending.

'The robbery took place at one o'clock yesterday morning. It was a fur warehouse – Svandal's. They're a Swedish firm with a depot here. Is Mixer the sort of man who'd be interested in furs?'

'Yes. It checks in with what Records know about him.'

'Good – that's another point. We're in luck, having you around. There were four men concerned and they drove up in two vehicles. One was a fifteen-hundredweight van and the other a saloon car. The watchman, William Hannent, has an office by the main gates. They told him they'd got a crate for him and coshed him when he came out.'

'How many men can he describe?'

'Only this man and another fellow. The other two were in ambush – they struck him down from behind.

'They opened the gates with Hannent's keys and drove the vehicles into the yard. There was no key to the inner store so they broke it open with fire axes. That's where the choice stuff's kept – the rest they didn't bother about. Hannent they left gagged and fastened to a chair. He was found there by the warehousemen seven hours later.'

'And the man on the beat – did he notice nothing?'

'They'd timed it too well. It was a pretty piece of planning. As a matter of fact, our man's on the carpet – he noticed Hannent was missing and did Fanny Adams about it. But then, of course, Hannent might have been on his rounds. We get precious little warehouse breaking in this part of the world.

'Well, that was the job that we were called in on, and Copping can tell you that it didn't bristle with leads. We guessed it was some city chummies and called up the Yard, but to date we've heard nothing from that direction.

'Then this morning we got a message from a man named Blaydon. He keeps a transport café on the Castra Road. He told us that at around eleven on the Tuesday night three men pulled up there in a fifteen-hundredweight Commer.

'They ordered a meal and sat down in a corner. He was able to give us a first-rate description of them. One of them was called Jerry and another one Polski, and he overheard a reference to "skins in the thousand-nicker class".

'At ten minutes past twelve they were joined by a fourth man. He was better dressed than the others and drove up in a green Citroen. He ordered a cup of tea and had five minutes conversation with them.

117

Then they left, the Citroen leading, going in the direction of the town.'

'You reported this to London?'

'Naturally. One would have thought that by now...'

'It wasn't much to go on. There's a lot of Poles in the fur trade.'

Gently sucked at his empty pipe, a wooden expression on his face. The more one heard of this, the more certain did it seem.

'This Blaydon – did he notice from which direction the Citroen was coming?'

'From town, which set us thinking that a local man was involved. Copping put on someone to check – there aren't so many Citroens in Starmouth. But there are only four green ones and this one was certainly green. Blaydon made a special note of it. He was surprised to see it pull in.'

'A pity he didn't make a special note of the number, too!' The super looked surprised, but went on with his account.

'By this evening, I have to admit, we were near the end of the road. Copping had double-checked every angle without un-covering anything fresh. Then your sergeant came to see us wanting assistance for the other affair, and as soon as Copping heard the description he knew he was on to something good.

'Especially when it came to the Citroen! That was the clincher in the business. We rang you at Hiverton directly, but unfortunately you weren't in. So, while the sergeant went to collect you, we fetched our witnesses and arranged a parade. Do you think it might be advisable to get on to London straight away?'

Gently hunched his shoulders sourly.

'First I think you'd better identify him. He's got an alibi of sorts – though he may not want to use it.'

'An alibi! Are you certain?'

The super sounded incredulous.

'One of the Bel-Air staff can vouch for him. He's supposed to have been there when you say he was in the café.'

Only now you could see right through it, that alibi of Mixer's. Against this latest information it was as transparent as tissue paper. It hadn't been for the murder: it had been for the robbery. That was why it didn't fit, why it had sounded mildly convincing. Maurice the bartender ... couldn't one see him pocketing the fiver?

'He won't want to use it.'

Gently bit at his pipe stem.

'There won't be any trouble about making

119

your job stick. But I'd like to see your witnesses – principally this Blaydon fellow. There's just an off-chance that he's got something for me.'

Blaydon was brought in, a thin man with narrow shoulders. He didn't seem a very good advertisement for his trade.

'It's quite right about the car, sir. I was washing up in my scullery. The window looks out on the road, as this gentleman can tell you.'

Gently went over it with care though he knew it was a forlorn hope. He had no reason to suspect what Blaydon was telling him. The man was just an average citizen who wanted to help – a little gratified, perhaps, by his momentary importance.

'When did you first see this car?'

'When it was coming along from the town direction.'

'What made you notice it?'

'It slowed down, you see. The man who was driving it was looking at my café I thought: "He won't stop!" – I only cater for drivers, really – but just then he made a turn and came sliding in to my pull-up.'

'Do you own a car yourself?'

'Yes, I've got a Ford "Pop"...'

'How many cars have you owned?'

'Well, five or six, one time or another.'

'Have you ever owned a Citroen?'

'No, I stick to English makes.'

'I'd like you, if you would, to describe the car that pulled in.'

In doing so he used terms which showed that the subject was familiar to him. One could hardly have pitched on a better witness for the description of a car.

'Of course it was dark at the time?'

'Yes, but I've got a big light over the pull-up.'

'Are you sure it wasn't a blue car?'

'No – green. It was a light-coloured green.'

'What else was parked in the pull-up?'

'Just a Leyland truck and the Commer.'

'Wouldn't they have hidden the other car?'

'No. Because of them he parked near my window.'

'Describe the man who came in.'

Without a shadow of doubt it was Mixer. His eyes, his skin, his accent: one could almost smell his sweat. He had tipped his hat to the three of them and ordered a strong cup of char. He had been wearing a dark blue suit and a matching wide-brimmed hat.

'Who else was in the café?'

'The driver and his mate from the Leyland.'

'Who were they – people you know?'

'They're from Brum … G.U.S., I believe.'

'Don't you have an assistant at the café?'

'Not after ten. It's just me and the missus.'

'Where was she when this man came in?'

'She was having her snooze in the room at the back. Ten till three, three till eight is how we work it. Then our man comes in and we both knock off.'

Mixer had paid for his tea and joined the others at their table. From their attitude it was clear that he was known to and expected by them. He pulled something from his wallet and laid it on the table. This they appeared to study while, keeping his voice low, he talked to them as though giving instructions.

At the end of five minutes they got up and left together.

'Why did you take so much interest in them?'

'As I said, he was a bit of an unusual customer. On top of that it seemed rum, him knowing those other three. They looked a rough lot and they didn't come from these parts.'

'From which direction did the Citroen come?'

'From the town way, from Starmouth.'

'You're quite positive of that?'

'As certain as I'm sitting here.'

Gently shrugged and picked up a sandwich, a plate of which had lately been put by him. There was no shaking evidence of this description: it was a bonus for any prosecuting counsel. And Mixer, if he'd come from Starmouth, was just about in the clear. He'd have had to go miles out of his way to avoid arriving by the Castra Road.

Unless ... dare one build any hope on it?

'Would you have been busy about then?'

'Not on a Tuesday. It's usually pretty quiet.'

'How long had you been washing up?'

'I don't know. Quarter of an hour, might have been twenty minutes.'

'And you were watching the road all the time?'

'You have to watch something on that job.'

'Did you see much traffic pass?'

'Not at that time on a Tuesday.'

'How many cafés are there on the Castra Road?'

'There's three besides me, one nearly into Castra.'

'Have they names and signs?'

'Only that one – the Blue Owl. The rest of us just stick up "call" or something.'

'I want you to think back very carefully, Mr Blaydon.'

Gently rocked forward on the back of his chair.

'This is very important and a lot may depend on it. Would you have seen that Citroen if it had first passed the other way – not appearing to slow down or take an interest in your café?'

Blaydon frowned for a moment or two in careful obedience, but the answer was plainly on the tip of his tongue.

'I'd have seen it of course, but I might not have noticed it. There were still one or two cars going back into town.'

'You didn't, in fact, notice it?'

'Can't say I did.'

'Or any other car in particular?'

'No, they were just cars.'

Gently let his chair sink slowly and reached for another sandwich. The case was still an inch or two ajar with regard to Mixer.

The identity parade was held in the canteen, this being the largest room at Starmouth Borough Police H.Q. Copping had supplied eleven stand-ins, five of them were policemen; at that time of night it was the best he could do, though at any time it would have been difficult to match Mixer. Gently watched the proceedings without enthusi-

124

asm. It was an open-and-shut case as far as the robbery was concerned. Neither witness was hesitant and Hannent swore at Mixer – the watchman's head was still bandaged, so his enthusiasm was understandable. The only interest now remaining was in Mixer's proficiency as a liar.

They returned to the super's office for the final act of the drama, Symms leading the way and Mixer urged on by Copping and Dutt. As usual the fellow was perspiring heavily, his mouth gaping open and his small eyes blinking. More than ever one wondered what a woman could see in him ... especially such a woman as Rachel Campion.

'Alfred Joseph Mixer, company promoter, of West Hampstead, Middlesex?'

He grunted some reply through his beak-like nose.

'It's my duty to warn you, Mixer – I daresay you know the formula. You're not bound to make a statement but if you do it will be taken down, and later it may be used in evidence. Have I made that perfectly clear?'

The super, quite visibly, was enjoying this part of the business. He had a relish for the details which bordered on the comic. Sitting upright behind his desk, he eyed the unhappy Mixer wolvishly; but he was being the classic model of an official accuser.

'I'm charging you that, on the morning of Wednesday, 7th August, in the company of three other men...'

In strictly regular phrasing the charge was rolled off. Mixer listened without reaction, unless it was the twisting of his hands. All the time his mouth hung open and his breath was sucked in hoarsely.

'...and that you then entered the premises of Messrs. Svandal at 54 Hammond's Quay, and removed from there furs to the value of thirteen thousand two hundred and thirty-six pounds ... have you anything to say in answer to this charge?'

'I wasn't there and I didn't do it.'

Mixer's croak didn't pretend to conviction. His eyes were wandering uneasily to Gently, as though seeking the answer to an unexpressed question.

'Would you like to tell us where you were?'

'I wasn't in Starmouth – not then, I tell you.'

'When weren't you in Starmouth?'

'Not when you says I was!'

'On Wednesday morning?'

'No – I left before then.'

In his corner the shorthand constable was deftly whisking it down. Copping, hovering beside the desk, rocked gently on his heels. He was studying Mixer through half-closed lids.

'I left there before twelve ... quarter to, it might have been. Then I just drove around a bit ... it was hot, like it is now. I just drove around to keep cool.'

'On your own, of course?'

'Yes ... no! I had a bit with me.'

'A woman, do you mean?'

'That's right, a bit of stuff. Said her name was Doris or something like that. On the bash, she was. I give her a quid for nothing.'

'Where did you meet her?'

'Somewhere ... a caff.'

'And you brought her back to Starmouth?'

'No ... she didn't live there.'

'Where did you leave her then?'

'I dunno ... where she told me!'

It was thinner than workhouse skilly, and Mixer must have been aware of it. The super was toying with him with a feline satisfaction. He didn't need to break the rules. It was superfluous to cross-question. One had only to keep Mixer moving to plunge him deeper in palpable falsehood.

'You say you did leave her somewhere?'

'That's right ... a village.'

'Which village was that?'

'How should I know which village!'

'Where did she tell you to go?'

'Not to no particular village at all. "Turn left", she says, "turn right" ... like that. It's no good asking me where we finished up.'

'What time did you leave her?'

'I dunno ... two, at least.'

'It took you over two hours from Star-mouth?'

'I didn't say that, did I?'

'Where did you go, then?'

'I went back to the Bel-Air at Hiverton.'

'You found your way back from this village, did you?'

'I – never you mind!'

Mixer broke off at last, vanquished by the sheer futility of it. Nobody was going to believe this, not even if he produced the woman! He licked his lips and stared sullenly at the floor. What he wanted badly was time to think the story over.

'That's all I'm going to say till I've seen my solicitor!'

The super shrugged. 'I'll want you to sign the statement.'

'I'm not going to sign nothing.'

'That's entirely up to you. Either way it's evidence and will be put in at court.'

Mixer's eyes flicked back to the bulky form

of Gently. Why had he been half-hoping that the Yard man would intervene? At the moment he'd got his back to Mixer and was fumbling with a package: he seemed to have washed his hands of the cockney, to have abandoned him to the Borough Police.

'I'm innocent, I tell you!'

Mixer's voice rose, thrilling with injury.

'I ain't done nothing particular – nothing! It's my hard blinking luck, that's all it is! I'm the last person on God's earth – the last ... the last...'

His voice trailed away as Gently swung towards him. Held mutely in the inspector's hands was Simmonds's painting of Rachel. A panel of flashing colour, it seemed to pulsate under the harsh neons. The wanton body of the woman glowed forth like a living question mark.

'That bloody little git!'

Mixer's face had gone pale with rage. His words came strangledly, incoherent with violent passion.

'*He* did that – didn't he – that's one of his! And she – she let him ... a little git like that!'

He raved in his anger, indifferent of who saw it. His hairy hands were clenched, his eyes bolting from their sockets. Of a sudden he made a spring at the painting, but Gently was too quick for him. Dutt, coming up behind, laid uncompromising hands on Mixer's person.

'I'll do for him, God help me – I don't care if I swing for it!'

He was foaming at lips which had turned a leaden colour.

'In the tent – that's one thing! This ... and him such a ponce! The next time I swear – when I get my hands on him! And she let him do it ... she let him do it!'

It ended almost in a sob. Mixer shuddered with a great violence. He sagged forward in the sergeant's grip and seemed as though he might have fallen.

'So you weren't jealous of her!'

Gently reversed the terrible painting.

'She was just your secretary – the one you liked to have around! And was that why you kept an eye on her? Was that why you assaulted Simmonds? Or is it usual for you to behave that way when it comes to a secretary?'

'You know why I didn't tell you!'

Mixer writhed in the suppressing arms.

'You'd have been on to me like a ton of bricks – I wouldn't never have stood a chance! I got a record, haven't I? I'm the bloke you'd try to pin it on. Put yourself in my place and ask yourself the question!'

'So you admit that she was your mistress?'

'My girl – that's what she was!'

'And you knew that she was unfaithful?'

'Can't you understand what it was like?'

Gently nodded. 'I know something about her – she could turn the head of any male. It wasn't just Simmonds, was it? He was simply the unlucky one. There were others from time to time, men you guessed about but never caught. That's the truth of the matter, isn't it – she had a lot of lovers?'

'Not the way you put it!'

'What difference does it make?'

'She was a good girl, that's what – a good girl. Can't you see it? If a bloke made a pass...'

'She wouldn't turn it up.'

'On account of that was her way – she couldn't bring herself to say no!'

Gently made an impatient gesture but Mixer wouldn't be put off. He struggled closer to the detective, thrusting his ugly face towards him.

'I'm not lying to you – it's the way she was made! It didn't mean nothing, see? She just couldn't help herself. And I'm honest with you – I was gone on her! Rachel was all the world to me. And she played the game ...

she did, I tell you! I'm not no bleeding catch, but because I was gone on her...'

'Was entertaining Simmonds playing the game?'

'She couldn't help it – it was just her nature.'

'And your nature to be jealous?'

'I ain't made of marble!'

'Yet you left her alone all Tuesday evening.'

Mixer drew back a little, his eyes searching Gently's. Twice his tongue went round his lips before he ventured on a reply.

'So I told Maurice to keep a watch on her.'

'Maurice? You mean the bartender?'

'He'd got the evening off – I gave him some money to stop around.'

'Wasn't he the one who gave you an alibi?'

'He didn't mean no harm by that.'

'In fact, what time did you get back to the Bel-Air?'

'It was half past two and that's the God's honest truth!'

Gently nodded again, this time more slowly. The super, at his desk, was pencilling notes on a pad.

CHAPTER SEVEN

There was no sign of the weather breaking on the Friday morning, and Gently, fresh from his shower, selected another of his amazing shirts. This time it was the filmstars' turn to have an outing. He spent a minute or two studying the effect in his wardrobe mirror. In front it was Miss Bardot in company with Miss Loren. Behind it was Miss Mansfield with Miss Dawn Addams. They had been portrayed, most probably, during just such another heatwave: they were sensibly dressed for it in light summer clothing. A garnish of palm trees assisted the composition, and the whole was carried out with a commendable vivacity.

When one was at Hiverton shouldn't one make a gesture?

Dyson had rung him early with compliments about the Starmouth business, but his lab report, touching the beach pyjamas, was next door to negative. Gently had himself rung Pagram at the Central Office. His colleague had sounded unhopeful and apologetic.

'We've worked back three addresses without turning much up ... she had a grandmother in Camden Town, if that's any help to you.'

'Is the grandmother still alive?'

'Give us time! We've only just heard of her.'

'You haven't got her surname?'

'No, it's very hearsay evidence. One of Campion's ex-landladies had it from another of her lodgers. Apparently he used to know Campion when she was living with her grandmother – we're trying to get on to him, but his tracks are a bit ancient.'

'Nothing about any parents?'

'Not yet, but we'll keep trying. The local records, incidentally, went up in the blitz; just one of the little things that make life easier.'

'What about her boyfriends?'

'There again we've had no luck. Since she joined up with Mixer she seems to have kept her nose clean. Before that, as you might expect, it's all rather vague.'

Gently told him about the warehouse raid, in which direction he had some hopes. If Mixer's gang was pulled in, an event not unlikely, then something might be elicited from one or another of them.

'I'll follow that up, naturally ... by the way, have you seen the *Echo* yet? In case you're at a loss, they've just solved the case for you.'

Gently had hung up and gone to collect the papers he'd ordered. Over coffee and rolls in the breakfast room he and Dutt browsed through them. Gently's braces and cheerful shirt figured on several front pages, but, as Pagram had hinted, it was the *Echo* which provided the highlight.

RACHEL CAMPION WAS MY MODEL!

The *Echo* reporter had scooped Simmonds. Following closely in Gently's footsteps, he'd dragged the self-same story from Simmonds's lips.

Nude Pose in Lonely Sandhills.
'Friend' Says Youth Who Left Home.
Police Seize Pictures.

It was all there except for mention of the thrashing. Detail for detail, it was what Simmonds had told Gently. Nor did one need to be a mind-reader to divine what the reporter thought about it – the murderer was Simmonds: it only awaited confirmation.

Yesterday I talked to John Peter Simmonds. We sat outside his tent on the remote Hiverton Sandhills. Two hundred yards away were drawn up the fishing boats. It was there, on Wednesday morning, that Rachel Campion was found strangled…

Facts, every one of them, and set down without comment; but how much could be inferred from facts put side by side like that!

In addition there was a picture of Simmonds standing at his easel, and a reproduction of a Rachel drawing which hadn't been in the satchel.

'Bloody little fool!'

Gently threw down the paper in disgust. Now the artist had really put his foot in it – there'd be no mercy for him from press or populace. Why hadn't the imbecile had the sense to keep his mouth shut? Instead, he'd poured it out to one of his worst enemies.

The rest of the papers had taken the Mixer angle and done their best to squeeze something out of it. They had got on to Blaydon and noticed the time factor: once, again there was no comment, but a naïve juxtaposition of facts.

Mixer was seen at Starmouth at twelve fifteen a.m. on Wednesday.

At Hiverton, seven miles away, Rachel Cam-
pion died between eleven p.m. and one a.m.,
according to police estimates.

But this was prosaic stuff beside the disclos-
ures of the *Echo*. From now on it was going
to be Simmonds who featured in the headlines.

The manager interrupted them, his
manner almost guilty:

'Those are two of my best rooms ... do you
think it might be possible?'

Gently had poked round Rachel's room
already, following in the footsteps of the
scientific Dyson. The local man had
performed prodigies in the matter of print
taking; he had also established that two
cigarette-ends had been the property of the
inmate. Mixer's room they had searched on
their return from Starmouth. It contained
nothing remarkable except some porno-
graphic literature.

'Tonight, probably...'

He left Dutt with the papers. Just once
more he wanted to look round that room of
Rachel's. In a very little while it would own
her personality no longer, like the scent of
cut flowers, it would have vanished away.

He unlocked the door, to be met by the

close smell of a shut-up room. Its windows faced seaward and admitted the morning sunlight. He went across and lifted the sash. The view comprised the lawn and tennis courts. Beyond them, over the marram hills, lay the dark, pacific sea; one could sit here counting the ships or watching the activities of the guests below. Mixer, of course, had had a similar prospect. His room was next door, though it didn't communicate.

'Fifteen-love!'

The youngsters were out already, bounding elastically around the courts. One could sense their exhilaration in the cool of the morning air. Over the lawn strode Colonel Morris, swinging a big Malacca cane. A moment later appeared the Midlands couple with their children and carrying towels. The inevitable record had just begun playing: it was a rendering of 'Long Black Nylons'.

And the room? That was simple enough, one took it in at a glance. A bed with shiny panels, wardrobe and dressing table to match, a bedside cabinet, three Lloyd Loom chairs, a cheap Indian carpet, and a candle-wick bedspread. By the bed stood her array of shoes, on the dressing table a silver-backed brush. In the wardrobe her clothes, gay, but not too expensive. In the cabinet

138

cigarettes and Mlle. Sagan's latest novel.

He took out the photographs and stood them up against the mirror. A little of that personality had started to filter through! The photographs had lied, or at best told half the truth. They had emphasized her sensuality and missed the human warmth behind it. She had been a friendly person ... wasn't that what stood out? Friendly, perhaps generous, perhaps even with a strength of character – allowing for a weakness, a failing not to be countered. Hadn't they each tried to tell him that in their separate, different ways? Simmonds, cleaving to the unexpected response, Mixer, grateful for her contradictory faithfulness? Yes ... a strength of character, an ability to go her own way. Sensual, promiscuous, but level-headed as well. A born and bred cockney, she was first of all a realist: she had accepted her life and produced something like a glow from it.

Wasn't that the true attraction, setting aside her physical beauty? Wasn't that what fascinated men even more than all the rest?

'Thirty-fifteen!'

Down below the game waxed furious. Racquets in hand, those waiting their turn stood by shouting advice and comment.

'Come into the net, Barry!'

139

'Whee! What a backhander!'

She had seen it all, heard it all, but now it went on without her. The essence of tragedy lay in other people's indifference.

Gently swept up the photographs with a sudden surge of violence. Who would have wanted to have killed her? What had she done to deserve that? Mixer didn't fit the picture – he was jealous, but he understood her. Simmonds? He was a better bet – a twisted little egoist. But there again, she'd been kind to him. She was a blend of mother and mistress. If Mixer had been killed that would've been another story ... as it was, what could have prompted a murderous fit in Simmonds?

He heard a movement by the door and glanced quickly towards it. Just too late a white jacketed figure glided silently out of view.

'Here... you! Come back a moment.'

Reluctantly Maurice reappeared. His expression was a little sheepish but otherwise he seemed at ease.

'Come in here – I want to talk to you.'

Maurice entered with his neat, graceful step. At close quarters one saw that he was not so young; there were fine lines meshing the corners of his eyes, a few white hairs amongst the sleeked dark brown.

'Take a chair, will you?'

'I should be in the kitchen.'

'Never mind that. You can refer them to me.'

Maurice shrugged delicately and took a chair beside the window. Rachel's bag was lying on it but he removed the obstruction without curiosity.

'I suppose you know why I want to see you?'

Gently himself sat on the broad wooden sill. The bartender's face was directly facing the sun: it was a perfectly calculated deployment for interrogation.

'It's about Mr Mixer, isn't it?'

'You didn't take long to guess.'

'Well, there you are – I knew it'd come out. It stands to reason that you wouldn't be satisfied.'

'Yet you told us a lie, didn't you?'

'I did my best for him.'

'How much did he pay you?'

'Fifteen quid altogether.'

This was frank to a point Maurice seemed rather to enjoy talking about it. His grey eyes nudged Gently's with a sort of confidential cynicism.

'It was a fiver to start with – did he tell you

about that? I was supposed to keep an eye on her while he was away in Starmouth. Then the next morning he sent for me and coughed up two more. That was to tell you he got in at a quarter after midnight.'

'And you told us – just like that!'

'I'd taken his money, hadn't I?'

'Didn't you realize that he might be Miss Campion's murderer?'

'We didn't hear about it till later, and then it was too late. Anyway, I reckoned that you'd soon have the truth out of him.'

There was no abashing the bartender by representing his iniquity to him. He obviously looked on Gently as a fellow *cognoscente*. Mixer had been tossing fivers about – good! Maurice had been in their way. It wasn't in human nature to have behaved any differently.

'And suppose I charge you with obstructing the police?'

'Go on! You wouldn't make a fuss about a little thing like that.'

Gently grunted but didn't press him. The time for that, perhaps, would come. He pulled out his pipe and filled it with deliberate slowness. The smoke curled bluely in the still, hot air.

'Tell me about Tuesday evening.'

'Tuesday?' Maurice grinned at him 'It's a long story, that is. How much do you want to hear?'

'All of it.'

'You'll get your money's worth. But it started before Tuesday. In a manner of speaking it started when she first set foot in the place.'

'What do you mean by that?'

'Can't you guess? I like the ladies.'

'You're telling me that you?'

'I wouldn't pass up a girl like Rachel!'

There was no hesitation about it – quite the reverse, indeed. Maurice revelled in the telling of his amorous history. He winked at Gently and made gestures with his head. When he came to the tit-bits he fairly rolled his tongue round them.

'I saw what she was the moment I clapped eyes on her – so could anyone else, if it comes to that. She'd got just that way with her – you know the sort? Every move, every jiggle ... and what a body she had!

'Her breasts were like melons and her thighs like trees, and sometimes she looked at you as though she wanted to eat you.'

Though he was properly behind the bar, Maurice had rushed to take up her baggage. He found her standing in front of her mirror

143

and taking the fastenings out of her hair.

'I nearly dropped a clanger. Mr Mixer was round the corner. She opened her bag to give me a tip, and I could see right down ... you get me? Luckily I heard him coming – but don't tell me she did it by accident!'

After that he was more cautious, though his lecherous mouth was watering. He watched and spied and made sheep's eyes at Rachel. She, too, had noticed him and gave him contemptuous encouragement. His sheep's eyes were caught and answered, and once or twice she was more provoking.

'Got me to run her bath and came in wearing next to nothing ... another time the bar was empty. She leaned on the counter and gave me a proper old eyeful.'

The moment came when the teasing was made up to him. Perhaps Rachel felt sorry for the tricks she had played. One evening she retired early, saying that the sun had given her a headache. Within twenty minutes she rang the bar asking for aspirins and water.

'Didn't Mixer suspect anything?'

'No, he was stuck into the *Record* – I'd just fixed him up with a nice long Scotch. Rosie took the bar for me – she's all right, is Rosie – and I went up the back way to keep it nice and unobtrusive.

144

'Guess how I found her? Stretched flat across the bed there! The light was out, of course, but it wasn't properly dark.'

'How long were you away from the bar?'

'Half an hour or forty minutes. I daren't stay longer, and perhaps it was just as well. As it was ... you understand me? I needed a brandy to pull me round. Rosie laughed her head off to see me looking so pale.'

'Where was Mixer when you got back?'

'Right there where I'd left him. He'd drunk another couple of whiskies but he hadn't left the bar. And for the rest of the evening...'

'When else did you make love to her?'

'There wasn't never another chance until Tuesday, worst luck.'

Gently relit his pipe while Maurice gabbled on. There was something absurd about this oversexed little man. He had the obscenity of a dog making public his amours: he couldn't be reticent, he had to talk about it too.

Yet Rachel had been attracted by him ... or amused, was it that? Had she been curious to make a trial of his superabundant amorousness? That would account for her provocations. She was probing him, trying him out. Maurice had amused her and she was deliberately applying the stimuli.

'All right – let's get to Tuesday.'

145

Maurice winked and shrugged his slim shoulders.

'It wasn't the way you think, but as a matter of fact I earned that fiver.'

'You went to bed with her again?'

'And that's just where you're wrong! She was upset about something and not in the right mood.'

They had come in late to tea, had Mixer and Rachel, and it was apparent to everyone that they had had a row. Rachel was looking sulky and sat very stiff and apart. Mixer's face was flushed and he growled ill temperedly at Rosie.

Throughout the meal they hadn't addressed a word to each other.

'After tea they both went upstairs, and Rosie heard them carrying on in here. She hadn't time to listen but she says they were proper angry. Mr Mixer was laying the law down and Rachel getting in a word now and then. Half an hour later he came into the bar. I was just getting things straight for Jimmy Simpson, my relief.

'"I want a word with you," he says, and opens his hand to show me a five-pound note. "They tell me you're off-duty, and I've got a little job for you. It won't give you a lot of trouble and it's worth what I've got here."

'I nearly had a fit when he told me what it was. It was all I could do to stop giving myself away. You might think it was a bit off, taking his money into the bargain; but then, I was a member of the union already. And if Rachel was with me she couldn't be somewhere else, could she?'

Fortunately or unfortunately, Maurice had been disappointed. Rachel's sulkiness had not diminished by the time she came down to supper. He no longer amused her. She had satisfied her curiosity about him. After the meal she fetched a book and went to sit with it in the lounge.

Then, at half past nine, she had a drink and went to her room. Maurice, following behind her, heard the bolt shot on her door.

'This was at half past nine, you say?'

'Give her ten minutes in the bar. I dare say it was closer to a quarter to ten.'

'And what did *you* do after that?'

'The best I could. I'm not one to pine.'

The best in this case happened to be Rosie, who had just finished in the kitchen. With a little persuasion she went into his room with him. There they entertained themselves till an early hour in the morning – which, exactly, Maurice wasn't able to say.

'Whereabouts is your room?'

'The one next to yours.'

'You wouldn't have heard Miss Campion go down again?'

'Not unless she wore hobnail boots.'

Gently smoked and brooded in silence. This was where the trail ended, at a quarter to ten. After that it was all surmise with very little to go on. She might equally well have gone out or stopped in her room ... unless the presence of her bag weighted the scales in the latter direction. If it did, who had persuaded her to unbolt that door?

'Did she have her bag with her when she went down to supper?'

'Can't say I noticed. It wasn't where my eyes were.'

'Did she usually have it with her?'

'Women don't go far without one.'

'All right. You can go now. Send Rosie up here, will you?'

Was there a tinge of uneasiness in those insolent grey eyes? Gently had deliberately hooked on the order to provoke some. But Maurice would hardly have given Rosie for an alibi unless he could depend on her: he rose jauntily from his seat, clicking his heels before he departed.

Rosie came in some five minutes later. She had had time to repowder and to dab on some scent. Closing the door, she favoured Gently with a truly blonde smile, and in sitting down she crossed her legs and leaned intimately towards him.

'What did Maurice say when he asked you to come up?'

'Maurice? He just said you wanted me in the bedroom.'

'What else did he say?'

She flickered her eyes coyly.

'He said you were a bit of all right, and that I needn't be afraid of you.'

'Just as long as I know!' Gently eased himself back a little. Rosie's perfume was oppressive and so was her person. She wasn't uncomely but there seemed to be a lot of her: when she talked she found it necessary to move a little closer.

'You remember last Tuesday, do you?'

'I don't see why I shouldn't.'

'Were you serving tea in the lounge?'

'Me and Betty were, between us.'

'Did you serve Mr Mixer?'

'Yes – he got on to me for spilling some tea.'

'What was his attitude towards Miss Campion?'

'Right-down nasty. You can take it from me.'

Gently's pipe was dead but he was obliged to get it going again. It was necessary protection against Rosie's affectionate incursions. Her face kept swimming up to him like a cheap-scented flower, and each time, by sensible degrees, she dragged her chair forward.

'How did you spend the evening?'

'Like one usually does here. After tea there was the supper to get, and then there's the washing-up. It isn't a rest-cure, I can tell you. We deserve our bit of fun.'

'You served Miss Campion at supper?'

'They sit at one of my tables.'

'What sort of mood would you say she was in?'

'She'd got a book with her but she didn't read much. Thoughtful, I'd say she was. Kept staring out of the window.'

'What did she do after supper?'

'I really wouldn't know. She went off out of the dining room and that's the last I saw of her. As it was I didn't finish up much before ten.'

'When you finished, what did you do?'

Rosie's face loomed up to within inches. She had painted her lips a pillar-box red, but a fine dew of perspiration had beaten the powder on her nose.

'Didn't Maurice tell you that?'

'I'd rather you told me.'

'You don't want a girl to give details, do you?'

'The facts and the times will do, I think.'

'Well!' Her lids sank modestly. 'I did spend a bit of time with him. You have to take your fun where you can get it, cooped up in a guest house. But you needn't think that just anyone … on the whole, I'm very particular! Only sometimes you get fed up with it, day-in, day-out.'

'Where did you meet Maurice?'

'He came into the kitchen looking for me.'

'At what time, did you say?'

'As near to ten as makes no difference.'

'And then?'

'Well, I had a wash – don't say I did a lot to myself! Then I went along with him, just like he told you. He was hanging about while I was having my wash – our rooms are next door, you see. They've put you in mine.'

'How long were you with him?' – Gently puffed voluminously. Rosie's knee was tentatively brushing his leg. 'I couldn't say, I'm sure! One doesn't really notice, does one? But it couldn't have been so late, because I had to get up in the morning.'

'About one say, or two?'

'Oh, not as late as that. When you have to

be down by seven you don't let things get out of hand. More like about midnight, that would have been it.'

'Are you sure about that?'

'I don't like to lose my beauty sleep.'

From outside they must be seeing this intimate *tête-à-tête*. Gently, his back against the window frame, was fairly cornered by Rosie's advance. Now she was leaning on the sill and gazing up into his eyes. Her face, in effect, was scarcely a pipe's length from his own.

'How long have you known Maurice Cutbush?'

With difficulty he slid from the sill and escaped into the room.

'Ever since I came here – Easter, that was. But he was here before that – two years, I think he said.'

'What are your impressions of him?'

'Oh, he's not so bad. He's been on the liners, you know, that makes them free and easy. From all accounts it was a poor trip when Maurice didn't get off.'

She had got up from the chair and was trailing him across the room. The moment he came to a standstill she seemed to be breathing down his neck.

'Has he got off with any other guests?'

'Dozens. That's how things go. In this sort

152

of business you get bored stiff – ask anyone you like. It's the same wherever you are.'

'And the guests make passes at you?'

'All the time, and some you wouldn't think.'

'Did Mixer ever make one?'

Indignantly she recoiled.

'As a matter of fact he didn't – but you've got to have your self-respect!'

Gently grinned to himself and struck a protective match. Rosie watched him re-provingly as he set it to his pipe. She was really trying hard – was it Maurice who had put her up to it? She couldn't believe yet that Gently was as coy as he pretended.

'Is that all you wanted to ask me?'

The match was out and she swayed to-wards him. For a moment her parting lips were tilted under his, her two firm breasts pressed lightly against him.

'It's my afternoon off ... I'm not doing anything. There's some things of mine I want to fetch from a drawer in your room.'

After she had gone he went back to the window. The lawn was now better tenanted and more deck-chairs were being fetched. An old lady with her knitting was casting furtive glances in his direction, but the majority of the baskers were still discussing their papers.

He relocked the door and slipped the key into his pocket. All the way down the stairs he was chuckling softly to himself.

CHAPTER EIGHT

The sun, by ten o'clock, was fully established, and the last of the morning had gone out of the day. The village and vicinity, which till then had seemed tolerable, now began to weary with its pitiless exposure. So little shade there was, so little promise of respite! Beach, marrams, and houses glared and rippled in the furnace. Not a motion stirred the grasses, not a bird sang anywhere. The air was a burden and one sweated doing nothing.

Oddly enough the effect was of darkness. The extreme brilliance of the sun appeared to vitiate colour. The sea looked heavy, the houses dulled, the sky itself seemed dusky and unluminous. It was the sun alone which throbbed with brightness. Into itself it drew again its effulgent light. Left behind was the heat, enveloping, ennervating: the world seemed plunged into a dark, fierce fever.

'Another scorcher!'

One heard it everywhere. With a peculiar emphasis, it expressed the weather exactly. And yet people were somehow proud of it, this Homeric bout of sun. Inevitably the two words would come out like a boast.

'Another scorcher, sir!'

Dutt had said it as they started out. The manager, too, had got it in when they passed him on the lawn. A little further on they encountered Colonel Morris. His step had lost its briskness and he had ceased to swing his cane.

'Another scorcher, eh? Reminds me of Alex!'

Why did they sound so personal about it, as though in some way it did them credit?

'That kid's in for a rough time, sir,' observed Dutt as they tramped along the beach. 'I haven't said nothing before, sir, but from the first I've had my doubts about him. I don't reckon we need worry about Mixer any more.'

Gently trudged ahead without replying. Everything was pushing the ball in Simmonds's direction. If you agreed to let out Mixer, then there seemed but one thing for it; yet, out of sheer pig-headedness no doubt, his mind kept shying away from Simmonds.

155

It was as if he had formed an equation the terms of which excluded the artist.

'There's his background, sir, you can't overlook it. The bloke on the *Echo* brought that out pretty well. Haven't we seen it before with kids like that? A little extra shove, and click! – they're over the edge.'

'You can't argue like that, Dutt.'

'I know, sir. But it makes you think. And like the paper says, she wasn't found far from his tent.'

Like the paper says! Was that what was influencing him? Not for the world would he have admitted it to himself. As always when on a case he made a point of reading the papers: sometimes they gave him a fact which he hadn't succeeded in eliciting. But he didn't let them bias him, one way or the other. They were a necessary evil which he had learned to put up with.

Besides, in this particular case ... there was Maurice, for instance. And even on the facts, those that one knew.

'You'd better tail him, I suppose, after we've had his statement.'

'It won't do any harm, sir, and might do some good.'

'He might do something silly. Let him see you around. If necessary I'll get another man out from Wendham.'

'He's the type to blow his gaff, sir, if he thinks we're really after him.'

As they drew nearer to the campsite the effect of the *Echo* article became apparent. Most of the people on the beach had gravitated in that direction. Except for a few small boys they didn't precisely stand and stare, but now and then a head would turn or a voice be cautiously lowered.

When the detectives arrived it was different: the crowd began to exhibit a purpose. From an accidental scattering they drew together in a group. They followed the two men up the sandhill and casually deployed themselves at the top – if this was to be the arrest, then nobody there was going to miss it!

'What are you doing with your tent?'

Simmonds was not alone at his campsite. On the hummocks round about were seated the reporters and their cameramen.

'I'm packing it up. I'm going!'

'Not today you aren't, I'm afraid.'

'But I am – I've got to! Can't you see what's happening?'

'You should have thought of that before you talked to the press.'

Already the tent was struck and partly packed away in a pannier. In another were

stuffed his blankets, while his gear lay together in a pile. A photographer, rising to
his feet, made an adjustment to his camera.
Simmonds started back involuntarily and
shrank behind Gently's protective bulk.

'You don't understand!'

'I do, I'm afraid.'

'I didn't know – I thought I could trust
him! He said I should put my story before
the public. I trusted him, I tell you! I didn't
guess for a moment.'

'I'm sorry about that, but you've got to
stay in Hiverton.'

'You wouldn't make me do it!'

'I can't let you do anything else.'

Persuasively the photographer sidled towards him. 'If you wouldn't mind turning...'

Simmonds threw up a terrified hand.

'They can't keep doing that – stop them! I
won't have it!'

The camera clicked smoothly, catching his
gesture and desperate expression.

'I can't stop here!'

He was pretty well in tears. His slight
figure was shaking as he stood helpless by
the ruined camp. From the crowd came a
motion which made Gently turn sharply. He
found himself staring into the burning eyes
of Bob Hawks.

'If you've got any feeling!'

'Very well. Finish your packing.'

'You mean you'll let me go?'

'No. Just do as I say.'

Everyone was straining their ears to catch the gist of what was passing. A few bolder ones had pushed forward, but the majority were holding their line. The reporters, however, felt no need for constraint; they crowded around chatting and trying to lever something out of Gently.

'You're going to detain him, are you?'

'He's going to sign a statement for me.'

'Where's he going then?'

'That has still to be decided.'

'He was her lover, wasn't he?'

'So far I haven't asked him.'

'It's a fact that you think he can assist you?'

'Everyone in Hiverton can be of assistance.'

From the corner of his eye he could see Hawks approaching. The fisherman was shuffling gingerly towards the centre of the circle. At a few yards distance he stopped, his lean frame slightly crouched: his gaze was fixed on Simmonds with a ferocious intensity of hate.

'Did you know he struck his father, and that that was why he left home?'

Nobody seemed to care whether Simmonds heard or not.

'We've been in touch with his ex-schoolmaster. He was noted for his violent temper. Once he struck a boy who was ragging him and knocked out a couple of teeth.'

The artist was trembling uncontrollably as he fumbled with his belongings. His hands were shaking so much that he could scarcely buckle the pannier-straps. From every side eyes were turned on him; the heat on the sandhill was terrific. At one time it looked as though he never would get those bags on.

'I've got n-nothing to put my paintings in!'

He turned towards them desperately, a pile of the canvases clutched piecemeal in his arms.

'You took away my satchel.'

'Dutt here will look after them.'

'Perhaps I can get some p-paper and string.'

He spilled two of them on the sand as he handed them to the sergeant. A reporter grabbed them eagerly, but they were only a couple of beachscapes. The crowd had fallen quiet and unnaturally still: one could well-nigh hear their breathing above the gentle wash of the combers.

'I'm ready to go.'

Simmonds heaved on the loaded cycle. Its wheels were burying in the sand and he had much ado to push it. The crowd shifted and murmured, but parted to make him way. It was Hawks, standing right in his path, who wouldn't budge an inch for him.

'You – murdering – little rat!'

He spat the words straight into Simmonds's face. One could feel, like an electric charge, the violence suddenly begin to generate.

'Hanging's too good for your sort – drowning in a sack'd be better! By rights we ought to string you up – here, where you did for her!'

It was trembling in the balance, that situation on the sandhill: in an ugly silence it was preparing to explode. A moment before the crowd had wavered between contempt and pity, but now, in a flash, the seed of hatred had been sown.

'There's only one thing for your sort!'

'That's enough from you. Get back!'

'I'll say what I please.'

'You'll get back out of the way!'

This was no time for argument, and Gently didn't argue. Poking his fingers into the fisherman's chest, he drove him backwards into the crowd.

'You two – Pike and Spanton! Take charge

of this fellow will you?'

Coming out of their stupor, they seized Hawks by the arms.

'Now take him away and see he doesn't cause more trouble.'

With surprising alacrity they marched Hawks off the sandhill.

It was enough to break the spell: the crowd had temporarily forgotten Simmonds. Their attention divided, they permitted him to depart. They watched him off the campsite in a sort of murmuring indecision: he was sobbing like a child and scarcely able to shove the bicycle.

The cameramen, in the meantime, had taken several excellent photographs.

The Police House was a building of stodgy brick which stood some distance inland from the village. It bore the date, on a tablet, of nineteen-thirty-five, and had a garage-like addition which was obviously a detention-room.

Mears was out when they arrived and they were received by his wife. She was a tall, raw-boned woman whose false teeth had a tendency to slip. She was nursing a baby and had another child in the garden. From her kitchen a smell of greens boiling was wafted through the house.

'We've a statement to take. May we use the office?'

She showed them through to her front room, which served the usual dual purpose. Across one of the corners was placed an old knee-hole desk. It bore a telephone, a Moriarty, a Kelly's, and the Starmouth directory.

'You'll find the forms and some paper.'

'Thanks. Don't let us disturb you.'

'I was wondering about a drink. I can soon fetch some lemon squash.'

Simmonds, at least, looked in need of refreshment. His cheeks were burning feverishly and his lips were dry as paper. Dutt had kindly wheeled the bicycle for him all the way through the village, but the artist was still trembling and much relieved to sit down.

'Now we'll just go over again what you told me, I think.'

He gave Dutt the desk and sat himself by the window. From there he could see, over Mears's lawn and hollyhocks, the road and the reporters – the latter having, of course, followed them. They were squatting in the shade of a tree opposite the gate. After a minute or two, as he knew they would, they produced a pack of cards.

'Please answer the questions slowly because the sergeant doesn't write shorthand. First give him your name, age, profession and address.'

His back was turned to Simmonds to give him a chance to recover himself. For the same reason he tried, where possible, not to interrupt the artist's answers.

'When did you first meet Miss Campion?'

Dutt would excise the superfluous verbiage.

'Where did you say she posed for this picture?'

'Which were the days on which she posed?'

Incoherent at the beginning, Simmonds gradually staged a revival. The even flow of the questions soothed him, coaxed him into a readier response. He paused to drink long draughts of the fruit drink which Mrs Meats had brought in. From where he sat he could see nothing outside except the pink and yellow heads of the hollyhocks.

'On the Tuesday afternoon.'

They were getting towards the end; the end, at least, of what Simmonds had told him.

'She left you where, you say?'

'On the beach near my tent.'

'And what did you do then?'

'I went up and got my tea.'

Gently paused, listening to Dutt's slow pencil go over the paper. When it came to a stop he swivelled round in his chair. Simmonds was sitting, glass in hand, looking much more collected: he even contrived to smirk at Gently with that ingratiating undertone.

'Where did you get that bruise from?'

'Bruise?'

'The one on your cheekbone.'

'Oh that ... on the tent pole. I hit it as I was coming out.'

'So it wasn't caused by a fist?'

'Fist? I...!'

Simmonds looked at him pitifully.

'Mr Mixer's fist on Tuesday afternoon – after he pulled you and Miss Campion out of your tent?'

The young man shivered and set his glass down on a cabinet near him. The blood was beginning to drain from his feverish cheeks. He made a fluttering movement with his hand, a sort of gesture that didn't materialize. He looked very much as though he wanted to be sick.

'I would have told you... I didn't think...'

'You didn't think that I'd get to hear about it?'

'No ... not that! It didn't seem important.'

'What was so trivial about it – when she was murdered a few hours later?'

Again that silly fluttering movement, this time with both hands. Really it was embarrassing to witness the artist's *mauvaise honte*.

'I wanted to tell you about it! Can't you see that? I want to tell you everything. I hate having to lie. But what would you think?'

'I think you can lie when it suits you.'

'But that's just the point! If you're going to take that attitude.'

The puzzle was that he sounded sincere in a naïve and curious way. One felt that he honestly did want to make a confidant out of Gently. The memory of another case flashed across the detective's mind, one in which, at his request, there had been a psychiatric examination. The subject there, a convicted sex-criminal, had shown much the same response. Only in his case they had known for a fact that the 'revelations' were crude romancing.

'You see, you can't help being a policeman, can you? By that I don't mean ... but there has to be a difference!'

'Never mind about that.'

'But I want you to understand...'

'What I want to understand is what happened on Tuesday afternoon.'

Here was another little surprise: Simmonds could talk about it freely. He needed only the slightest prompting to give them a fully-rounded account. It was as though the whole thing had been waiting on the tip of his tongue – sometimes Gently had to slow him for the benefit of the toiling Dutt.

'It was she who suggested it, going into the tent. She knew I wouldn't have dared ask her – it hadn't been like that, you know! There wasn't anybody about, except some cars on the track. I don't know why she did it unless it was to pay me for the painting.

'And in fact, I hardly had time to do up the ties.'

It all checked neatly with what Gently had been told, allowing for some softening of the facts about the beating. In Simmonds's account this wasn't quite so one-sided: he had exchanged a few blows before Mixer knocked him down.

'What was Miss Campion doing?'

'Naturally she tried to stop us. She kept calling Mixer a brute and telling him not to be a fool. But in spite of his size, if my foot hadn't slipped...'

'She went off with him, did she?'

'Yes, he *ordered* her to go with him.'

'And that was the last time you saw her?'

'The last time ... until...'

Now it was difficult to stop him from elaborating the details. His awkwardness had gone and he was even picking his words. A great load, you would have thought, had been lifted from his mind: at last he could tell it all, he could spill it out freely.

Why then was Gently's face growing glummer and glummer ... why did he return to the window and stare unseeingly at the hollyhocks?

'There ... I think that's everything. If you've got it down I'll sign it. I don't want you to think ... but you know I would have told you! Honestly, I'm not one to tell lies as a rule.'

'Just one more question.'

Gently's shoulders were hunched. There was a deadness in his voice which made Dutt look up quickly.

'Amongst all the rest of it you seem to have forgotten something. We know when Miss Campion left you ... but what time did she come *back?*'

Simmonds was wretchedly sick and had to be taken to the bathroom, a proceeding which greatly concerned Mrs Mears. She fetched a flask of brandy from a chest in her bedroom, and seemed half in a mind to give

168

Gently a lecture.

'Why don't you let him be for a bit?'

Gently thanked her but made no comment. He sat at the desk, ruffling through the leaves of Kelly's; he seemed quite unperturbed by the artist's latest calamity.

'Feeling better, are you?'

The inquiry was academic. Simmonds's face wore a greenish tint and he shivered now and again. He sat half doubled-up, his arms folded across his knees: his attitude was one of the completest dejection.

Gently relinquished the desk and returned to his previous seat. Under the tree the reporters were still busy at their cards. They had been joined by a straggle of the curious from the beach, and occasionally one or another of them threw a quick glance at the Police House.

'You couldn't know about that!'

The artist's voice was a mumble, and after he'd said it he was stricken by a fit of the shivering.

'It was dark ... there was nobody ... nobody could have told you! You're guessing about it, that's all you're doing.'

'But it's true all the same.'

'Not unless I say so!'

'Whether you say so or not. I know too

much about her.'

'But you couldn't know that!'

'It's simple enough, isn't it? Being Rachel, she came back: she wasn't the *sort* to let you down. Especially after Mixer had thrashed you, right underneath her eyes.'

'But you've got to have proof!'

'That's what you can give me.'

'I won't ... ever...'

'Hadn't you better think it over?'

Simmonds covered his face and began to sob. It was the only sound in the overhot room. Dutt succeeded Gently in his researches into Kelly's; his senior sat motionless, his eyes fixed on the group of card-players.

At the door, in all probability, Mrs Mears was indignantly eavesdropping.

'You'll think it's all lies.'

Gently smiled grimly to himself.

'I'd tell you ... but now ... and everyone's against me. Whatever I say.'

He choked himself with sobbing.

'Suppose I confess ... are they certain to hang me?'

But it was less than a confession when it came to the point, though, if it were true, one could understand the hesitation. Slowly it came out, interrupted by sobbing: Simmonds ran truc to form and didn't need to be led.

'It's true ... she came back. It was about ten o'clock.'

When, of course, it was dark enough to conceal where she was going. She had got rid of Maurice – did she guess he'd been set to spy on her? – and let herself unobtrusively out of the Bel-Air. Then she had hastened along the beach, which one could depend on to be deserted, and climbed up the sandhill to where Simmonds was nursing his bruises,

There she had remained about an hour, if Simmonds was to be believed. She left just after eleven, returning by the way she had come. Simmonds had gone directly to bed. He admitted that he hadn't slept well. At some time in the morning, not long after he had heard the boats come in, he had risen with the intention of having a swim before breakfast.

'You'll never believe me ... what's the use of going on?'

'You saw her, then, did you, lying between the boats?'

'No! That's why it's impossible ... she wasn't near the boats.'

'Where was she then?'

'Right there ... in front of the tent.'

He wasn't far wrong in anticipating disbelief – Gently stared at him for a long time without opening his mouth. It was an odd sort of tale to tell if Simmonds were guilty, on the other hand, murderers sometimes told an odd tale.

'In that case, how did she get down to the boats?'

'I took her there.'

'You did!'

'What else could I do? If someone else found her...'

'Why did you leave her by the boats?'

'I couldn't get her any further. She was too stiff and heavy ... it was making me sick.'

Gently let him stumble on through the rest of his narrative. There wasn't much to add to it which was to the artist's credit. He had slunk back to his tent and tied the flaps to behind him; he'd lain trembling and fearful, even getting back again into his blankets. In an ecstasy of terror he had heard Nockolds approaching. The terrible barking of the dog had warned him that the body was discovered.

'I've always hated dogs ... always ... always!'

It was a long time before he dared to join the crowd on the beach.

'Exactly where was that body?'

'In front of the tent. I could show you.'

'How far away?'

'It was' – Simmonds trembled – 'it was just where that man was standing, the fisherman ... his feet.'

'In which direction was it pointing?'

'The head was pointing towards my tent.'

Dutt read over the statement and Simmonds scrawled a signature to it. The whole business had taken them little over an hour. In her kitchen Mrs Mears had brewed an urn-like pot of tea; it was strong and made so sweet that one could nearly stand up a spoon in it. The greens, providentially, had been removed from the stove, though their odour yet clung to the sweltering atmosphere.

'Where – where are you going to take me?'

Simmonds had an air of docility, a meekness that suggested a well-spanked child.

'Nowhere. You're free to go. Just stay around Hiverton.'

'But I thought...'

'Well you were wrong! Only don't try anything foolish. If you take my advice you'll find some digs in the village. Your stuff can stay here until you're ready to collect it.'

'Then you really believe?'

'Don't be too sure of that.'

Simmonds shook his head bewilderedly and gulped down the syrupy tea.

At the door there was another crisis – for the first time he saw the reporters. They had risen to their feet and were shuffling together cards and money. Simmonds went a few steps and then came to a standstill, a spasm of violent trembling overcoming his slight body.

'I can't go – you mustn't make me!'

He turned in a panic to where Gently stood.

'I'd rather be arrested ... please! I'd rather...'

'Unfortunately I haven't given you the option.'

'If you like I'll confess ... please, don't make me go!'

In the end Dutt went off with him, as an alternative to tailing. Mrs Mears had supplied him with the address of a likely lodging. To the last he kept looking back hopefully towards Gently, but the figure which blocked the doorway steadily refused to catch his eye.

CHAPTER NINE

Was there a tempest brewing out of all that heat? Gently had several times glanced at the innocent-seeming sky. The air had a hectic feel and the sun was brassy; a lot of ugly black flies had appeared and were fluttering about everywhere. Thunder-flies, were they? They had the appearance of evil. Their legs were long and shining and their antennae flickered ceaselessly. But as yet there was no sign of thunder, not a scratch on the dusty heavens. Today was like yesterday and probably tomorrow – another scorcher. What could improve on that description?

He dropped in at the Beach Store to buy himself an ice cream. On his way through the village he had encountered a group of fishermen. They were lounging under a wall and smoking their short clay pipes: they watched him in a heavy silence as he drew level with and passed them. Then one of them had spat – had the timing been coincidental? Bob Hawks was one of their number, but like the rest he'd held his peace.

Mrs Neal, too, seemed unfriendly, or at least indisposed for a chat. She had gone straight back to her other customers after she had made his ice cream, though they, like Gently, were served and merely passing the time. He went out feeling that she had let him down in some way. It was possible that she thought he had inspired the article in the *Echo*.

He followed the example of the fishermen and found a wall under which to sit. He wanted time to think the business over, to try the pieces in their varying patterns. He had a case against the artist, of that there wasn't a shadow of doubt. If it went before the public prosecutor then a suitable indictment would have to follow.

Only – and here he was back at the beginning – the case against Simmonds didn't satisfy Gently. Somewhere, somehow, it was failing to click: it was jarring against deep-seated, deeply felt intuition. But what was that intuition and how had he come by it? Alas, that was the very thing which Gently didn't know. All that he could do was to worry over the facts and to try, once more, to evolve something fresh from them.

He pulled out the notebook which he kept for unofficial musings. Finding a clean page with difficulty he began to scribble down the situation. There were four of them in it, beginning with Mixer, though the connection of the fourth suspect was tenuous indeed:

(1) A.J. Mixer. Motive: jealousy.
   Opportunity: possible.
(2) J.P. Simmonds. Motive: psychopathic.
   Opportunity: considerable.
(3) M. Cutbush. Motive: psychopathic.
   Opportunity: good.
(4) R. Hawks. Motive: ? Opportunity: ?
Note: if Simmonds tells the truth somebody may be trying to frame him.
Note: Hawks's behaviour towards Simmonds.

Having got that down he lit his pipe and stared at the scribbling. Then he added, as an afterthought:

Does Dawes know something about Hawks?

Over this he brooded for some time, making little marks with his pencil, but finally he drew two lines under it with a sort of conclusive emphasis. Whether Dawes knew something or not, nothing would ever draw it out of him. He might inform on a stranger like Simmonds but he would never shop one of his own 'subjects'.

And then, what was there to be known about the evil-tempered fisherman? Gently couldn't begin to guess, it was the thinnest part of his summation. On rational grounds alone Hawks could scarcely be said to come into it. There wasn't the merest suggestion that he had any connection with Rachel.

And yet...

Gently hovered again over the pencilled name with the (4) beside it. Wasn't that the direction in which he found himself being drawn? If any single thing was making him hesitate about Simmonds, then it was the look which Hawks gave the artist that morning on the sandhill. A look ... against a comfortable fileful of evidence!

He grunted and shoved the book back in his pocket. It was time he put the fisherman out of his mind. There was a more logical outsider to be had in Maurice – and Mixer, he still wasn't exactly in the clear!

Suppose he had come back and caught Rachel leaving the tent – was it too much to suppose that he'd gone there looking for her?

Gently got to his feet and brushed himself irritably. With a clear case to present he felt more in the dark than ever. The trouble was that he wasn't content to be a simple chief inspector: he wanted to be the jury too, and probably the appeal court on top. But it wasn't his business to say whether Simmonds was telling the truth.

Why couldn't he let it rest there, and leave the artist to take his chance?

The heat made it a penance to be on the beach, and it may have been as a penance that Gently plodded down there. He had no hopes of a sea breeze – Hiverton despised meteorology – and the lapping of the waves was not an invitation for him.

At the net store he passed Dawes, armed today with a telescope. The owner of the *Keep Going* didn't acknowledge Gently's stare. His blue eyes gazed ceaselessly towards the haze-misty horizon, and he seemed quite untroubled by the stark beating of the sun.

Nor were the visitors much troubled by it, judging by their activity. Only a few of them, the elderly ones, sat in the shade of the boats. The usual crowd of youngsters were swimming and playing on the beach, others lay tanning, a few were amusing their children. Near the gap stood an ice cream stall which was doing a steady business. A portable radio was playing under a sunshade lower down.

Had they forgotten about it, then, that earlier scene on the sandhill? One would almost have thought so, strolling among them now. Separated into units they were reasonable people, ashamed, very probably, of their madness of that moment. Nevertheless they had made a mob, these reasonable people. With a scapegoat set before them they had been ready enough for violence. Had they seen in Simmonds something a little too germane, something too much like themselves to be viewed with strict sanity?

But they were reasonable people ... now, at all events! They were basking in the sun and congratulating themselves on the weather. If they glanced uneasily at Gently that was only to be expected: they didn't really want a policeman cluttering up their pleasant beach.

He tramped down to the foreshore where the children were paddling and building castles. A number of them had banded together and were digging quite a sizeable hole. A boy of seven or eight was trying to float his model yacht; it must have been ballasted wrongly because it persisted in turning turtle.

The sea ... hadn't that to do with it, in some incomprehensible way? The sea which Dawes kept watching, as though it held an unutterable secret?

He turned his head to look for the man. Yes, he still stood there. As upright as one of the posts, for all his sixty summers, he remained planted by the hut in his tireless, oblivious vigil.

But what was he looking for in those acres of changeful water? Perhaps he couldn't have told you himself; though you caught him in the mood. They were a 'rum lot', fishermen, they didn't work like other people. Even here, in their native village, they were a race apart from the others. A fisherman's wife was a fisherman's widow. They were a right 'rum lot', and nobody understood them.

Except one of themselves ... you could be certain of that! Within the clan they would understand each other, better than did the people outside it. Together in work, together in danger, together in that inexpressible communion of the sea ... they were more like a band of brothers, a religious order almost: they were the receptacle of secrets past common understanding. And to share them you must belong, to partake of the revelation; after which ... wasn't it possible? ... you could murder and get away with it!

Gently shifted his feet in the baking shingle. It was true: one could probably get away with murder. Dawes wouldn't split on Hawks though he caught him red-handed – it was a fisherman's murder, so let who would swing for it. The sea washed away all the sins of its children.

Again he looked back at the figure on the sandhill. Was it just an illusion, or was Dawes now watching him? The tilt of the cap seemed a few degrees lower, the head was turned a little from its original eyes-front. Impulsively, Gently began to walk towards the net store. There was no harm in trying even though Esau wouldn't answer him. Sometimes silence was expressive, some-times more so than loquacity; it wouldn't be the first time that Gently had drawn blood from a stone.

But then, half way up the beach, he came to a puzzled halt. Dawes was no longer posted there like a storm-beaten figurehead. The net store was deserted. There was no-body within yards of it. The fisherman had vanished as though the sandhill had swal-lowed him up.

The disappearance of Dawes had something less than canny about it, because Gently had been watching the man all the way from the foreshore. Only once had he glanced away –

when his toe stubbed a pebble – and it was in that fraction of an instant that the phenomenon had taken place. He hurried eagerly up to the store, into which Dawes might have slipped. Had the door been unlocked he would have had bare time to do it. But no, it was bolted and the padlock in position: there was nowhere at all where a man could have hidden himself.

Then a movement caught his eye in the direction of Simmonds's campsite. As mysteriously as he had vanished, Dawes had quietly reappeared! Half-concealed by one of the tops, he stood with face averted from Gently; in his demeanour there was no sign that anything out of the way had occurred.

Yet he must have moved like a goat ... how else could he have covered so much ground? The distance was upwards of a hundred yards and, to keep out of sight, he must have run doubled...

Cautiously, Gently began to approach him, but immediately Esau sank down out of sight. By the time Gently himself arrived at the campsite his quarry was once more a hundred yards away. What was the man's object? Was he having a game? There hadn't seemed very much gamesome about Esau. As Gently paused, so too did the fisherman:

he became again the sea-staring statue.

Gently compressed his lips and plodded steadily forwards. There was only one way to see what this was all about. If Esau wanted to play games, well, he was going to have his chance. When it came to *this* sort of game, Gently wasn't entirely an amateur!

Soon there wasn't any doubt about Esau's intentions; he was deliberately leading the detective up the marrams. When Gently hurried, he hurried. When Gently stopped, he stopped. And always, without looking round, he kept at the same approximate distance. Before long Gently found himself grudgingly admiring the fellow. He began to perceive what it was that impressed the other fishermen. Esau was tough and he was clever, but he was something else besides. There was more than the look of a Viking about that active, bearded figure.

And what a chase he was giving Gently under the biting, sucking sun! On the beach, over the tops and through the spiteful, heart-breaking marrams. There was no settled line of country. Esau went just where his fancy took him. Now they were up, now they were down, now they were battling through furze and scrub. One thing, however, was clear. They were drawing further and further away from the village. The last scatter of visitors was quickly left behind them; for the rest, they were alone with the sea and the marrams.

At one point Esau stopped and seemed to stamp with the heel of his sea boot. The pause was only momentary and he was away before Gently could get there. The spot was a shallow depression, like many others, in the top of a sandhill; the mark of the sea boot showed quite plainly, but there were also some other marks.

So Esau knew about that too – he knew the spot where the painting had been done. Gently had only to glance at the place to know why his attention had been drawn to it. Undisturbed, for there had been no wind, was the impression of a reclining body; at a distance of six feet from it were impressed the marks of easel and stool. Rachel, apparently, had been a little bored. She had played with the sand and burrowed her feet in it. Near Simmonds's easel there were dark-coloured stains – where, one imagined, he had emptied his dipper.

And Esau knew ... because he had watched them? Gently's glance switched curiously after the evasive fisherman. He was waiting there at his customary distance, his face, inevitably, towards the sea. And at the first suspicion of movement from Gently, he was off again on his singular travels.

The man from the Central Office scrambled after him cursing. If Esau wanted to tell him something, why these round-about methods? They must have put in miles on those everlasting marrams, and a cheap pair of sandals weren't the equal of good sea boots. But Esau was the boss, and there was nothing to be done about it. If Gently wanted to maintain contact then he was obliged to tag along. His lonely conso-lation was that Esau had a method – they were on their way towards something, though what it was he couldn't guess.

In the end, did Esau take a little pity on him? Their advance, at last, became more direct; he was straying less off the path as they approached the sandhill that marked the Ness. It loomed before them, a veritable giant, a miniature mountain among sand-hills. Lying athwart the line of the others, it reduced the best of them to insignificance. Its sides were as steep as house roofs, it bettered a hundred feet at least. Gently, dashing the sweat from his eyes, was praying that Esau didn't mean to climb over it.

But Esau did, that was soon apparent.

Gently could tell it from the way he marched up to the obstacle. The sea boots, never pausing, thrashed on up the pitiless slope, dislodging puffs of dusty sand as the toes stabbed out their holds. Really, that hill was a little too much! One ought to be content to go round by the beach. Arriving at the bottom just as Esau got to the top, Gently planted his feet like an obstinate horse. His whole attitude was eloquent of his intention to stay there.

And Esau? For once he'd got his eyes off the sea, he was sitting down calmly and lighting his pipe. He, too, had expression written large in every line of him: We're here, it said, now what do you make of it?

Exactly!

Gently shook his head and seated himself; likewise. He could think of one reason only why Esau should bring him here. It was because, being here, he couldn't be also in the village, though why Esau should want that was a deep-sea mystery. Anyway, he'd got it and where did they go from there?

They didn't go anywhere was what Esau seemed to say. From the fact that he'd lit his pipe you could assume that this was the spot. And he wasn't looking at the sea, if that was any help. He was sitting there smoking and looking ... straight below him.

The significance of this didn't strike Gently for a moment, then, because it was continued, he followed the line of the fisherman's gaze. It was fixed on a certain hollow lying close to the foot of the sandhill, a hollow in which was growing a clump of the omnipresent marram grass.

Gently rose to his feet again and wandered over to the hollow. It was about thirty feet in diameter and as symmetrical as a basin. The sides and floor were of smooth sand and bore little vegetation; at one point the edges were broken as though there somebody had been in the habit of descending. The clump of marram grass was growing exactly in the centre. It was a handsome, clean-growing colony and occupied a small mound. The effect of the whole was that of a rather neat bomb crater – which, very likely, was just what it was.

But why did Esau want to draw his attention to a bomb crater? He looked up at the brooding figure in the hope of receiving a sign from him. But there was nothing to be had there: Esau sat silent and monumental: his solitary gesture was his meditation on the hollow.

Gently moved a little closer and began a

more careful scrutiny. From the surface of the sand he could tell that nothing recent had occurred there. Everywhere it had a hard crust and bore the marks of pelted rain – rain which, he remembered, had happened three weeks ago; it was the storm which had precursed the onset of the dry spell. Apart from that there seemed little to see, except the antics of a pair of lizards. The crater was empty of everything but heat.

After all was it a joke that the fisherman was playing on him? Gently frowned through his sweat as he stumbled round the circumference. Nothing had happened here, at least while Rachel was in Hiverton, and the indications were slender of anything having happened before that. Then what was he looking for – what was the point of it? Didn't it rather bear the stamp of Esau's unusual sense of humour?

Just about to give it up, he came to a sudden, alerted halt. That grass! Surely there was something out of the ordinary about that? It didn't have the rough look of the tangles round about; it was tall and clean and straight – one would almost have said it was cultivated.

And more ... it had shape. Gently shifted the better to see it. Once you tumbled to the idea, it was easy enough to trace a design. The clump of grass was shaped like a cross: it was crude, but it was definite. One of its arms was longer than the others ... it was, in fact, the cross of the Church!

Certain now that he'd grasped the meaning, Gently glanced up for confirmation, but the fisherman was no longer staring down at the hollow. He was still perched above, but his head was turned seaward. His vacant blue eyes were once more on the horizon.

And Gently found himself shivering in the midst of the pounding heat: shivering as though cold water had been trickled down his spine. For a moment he stood uncertain, his eyes fascinated by the cross of grass; then he turned his back with an effort and began to hurry towards the village.

Mears was sitting in his shirtsleeves when Gently re-entered the Police House. He got up immediately and did his best to look official.

'Where's your record of missing persons?'

'Missing persons? We haven't got any.'

'Don't you lose a fisherman sometimes?'

'W'yes, they get drowned now and then.'

Mears departed into his office and returned carrying a manila folder. Gently, drumming his fingers with impatience, could hardly wait to have it undone.

'Two years ago ... that was the last one. The *Rose Marie* got run down by a drifter. Then there was the *Girl Sue* in the March of 1954. She struck a mine off Hamby. I heard the bang myself.'

'But individual fishermen?'

'Gone missing, do you mean, sir? There's only one, Sid Gorbold – and that wasn't any mystery. He was paying a maintenance order and skipped a drifter at Peterhead.'

'And there's nobody else missing?'

Mears was positive that there wasn't. He'd been constable at Hiverton since August 1935, and could remember no authentic case of a person going missing. Gently listened to him moodily: he'd been toying with a theory. But there was no reason to doubt the information of Mears.

'Have you got a couple of spades?'

Mears fetched a pair from his tool shed. He was doing his best to conceal a natural curiosity.

'I'd like another man, and I don't want to go through the village. Is there a way round the back here which will take us on to the marrams?'

Nockolds was impressed for the party – he

didn't like to refuse them – and Mears led the way over some meadows and rough pasture. Gently plodded along silently, without offering an explanation. At the back of his mind there was still a feeling that the fisherman might have been fooling.

When they came to the giant sandhill Esau was sitting there no longer. The hollow, undisturbed, lay shadowless under a vertical sun. A noonday peace entranced the place and it had an air of enormous distance. The only sound was the maundering of the sea which wafted softly across the dunes.

Gently turned to the gaping Nockolds:

'You're no stranger in these parts! Take a look at that clump of grass there – how long have you noticed it growing like that?'

But Nockolds had never noticed it, and he didn't notice it now. To him it was just another clump, like a hundred million others.

'Right – start digging underneath it.'

They shed their jackets with little enthusiasm. The heat coming out of that hollow had to be experienced to be believed. Gently, hands in pockets, stood over them in a slave-driving attitude. He could see, what he might have guessed, that digging out a marram clump was hell.

'How far do you want to go down, sir?'

192

They were grunting at every spadeful and Nockolds, in a thick twill shirt, was already showing signs of distress. Mears was being braver about it: he had a sense of duty to support him. In putting the question to Gently he strove to keep a neutral tone.

'Just keep going until I tell you.'

They fell to again with savage purpose. The marram clump was churned and scattered, its fibrous roots thrown up to the sun. Beneath it the sand was moist and darker, it clung to the spade and made neater digging; but it was firm and it was settled, it hadn't been disturbed for years. Gently's face grew steadily longer as he watched each successive spadeful.

'Someone's been here before, sir.'

Mears was the first to notice the signs: he leaned on his spade, the sweat pouring down him miserably.

'There aren't any layers, sir, like there is where it's natural. The sand's all mixed together ... there's been a hole here before.'

'Before – but how long?'

Mears scratched his head expressively.

'Ten years or fifty, you can't say more than that.'

But now they worked with more intentness – it wasn't a mare's nest, after all. Someone had been that way ahead of them, however far ahead it had been. With a certain obstinate eagerness they delved on under the caning sun.

'What's that you've got your foot on?'

At a depth of five feet they found it. By then the heaps of sand had risen higher than their heads. The sand had started to come out grey, it had been grey for the last five minutes. Nockolds, stepping back for a stretch, had set his boot on something that crunched.

'Bones!'

He shifted his footing in a hurry. Mears, too, shuffled aside with alacrity. Gently came skidding down the wall of the hollow, his sandals burying in chill, soft sand.

'You come out – leave Mears to finish it.'

'Blast, but I'd never have thought...'

'Come on out! You've done your job.'

Shaking a little, the poacher climbed out of the excavation. During the rest of the proceedings he sat, looking sick, on one of the heaps. Gently, getting down on his knees, directed Mean's operations. In the end they were both of them scooping away in the hole.

'A bit small for a man is it?'

The skeleton lay strictly oriented. The hands, with the fingers entwined, had been placed correctly across the breast. A yellowish staining had occurred due to contact with the sand. There remained some traces of shoes, but the clothes had rotted away.

'More like a woman ... a boy, at least.'

In life, the skeleton's owner had probably measured around five feet seven.

CHAPTER TEN

If it was any consolation to Gently, he had lost the reporters' attention. To a man they had attached themselves to Dyson and his colleagues. Here was bigger and better news – a second body found at Hiverton: already one could see the headlines staring brashly from the morning editions. One could guess, too, the speculations. If two bodies, then why not three? Had they come to the end of it yet, or were there grim finds still to be made? THE VILLAGE OF DEATH – A REIGN OF TERROR! – it was working up to that. A little benevolence by the god of scribblers, and a whole clutch of bodies might invigorate the 'story'.

Probably a dozen newshawks now swarmed in the little village. Dyson had brought in extra men to try to cope with the situation. Superintendent Stock had driven over in his highly polished Humber; he had conferred with Gently over lunch, but in effect there had been only one question:

'Do you think there's some connection?'

If only there'd been a convincing answer! And to his second query, 'How did you find it?', Gently had had nothing to say that wasn't evasive. Esau he wanted entirely on his own – there was nothing to be gained from throwing him to the county police. The Sea-King would know nothing, say nothing, admit nothing. His assistance had been shadowy and he would certainly disclaim it.

So the super had gone away feeling dissatisfied with Gently; the fellow was holding out on him, it was plainer than a pikestaff. Dyson, too, had seemed resentful, though he was still reproachfully co-operative. During lunch he had twice phoned in to provide the latest progress reports.

'It's a woman, we're sure of that, though we don't know how she died. The bones seem to be intact and there aren't any injuries to the skull. I've got a man taking samples of sand to see what we can recover ... she's been dead above twenty-five years: Simpson won't go any closer than that.'

'Has he any idea of her age?'

'Between twenty-five and thirty-five. She was five seven and a half and her hair was darkish and worn short. She'd had some dental treatment, but we'll be lucky to do anything with that ... for the rest, we're checking back on the H.Q. files of missing persons.'

The second call gave the result of this. It was altogether negative. On a check that went back to nineteen-twenty they had discovered nobody who fitted the facts.

'We're getting on to Norchester, Starmouth, and Lynton. If they can't help us we'll try Lewiston and Southshire.'

'Have you been in touch with Records?'

'Yes, we're sending them the dental data. I suppose you've got nothing to add which might shed a little light?'

Gently's mood ever since the discovery had been one of curious suspension. It seemed to have paralysed his interest in everything that had gone before. The change defied his present analysis. It presented itself in the form of an analogy. It was as though, until now, he had been walking in a certain landscape; and that suddenly the light had altered, and everything had altered with it. Altered, but was still the same! There lay the enigma that baulked his comprehension. The objects composing the landscape were each still in their place, but now, in this new light, they had secretly varied their significance.

And as suddenly he felt cut off by this novel shift of vision. He had moved into a different world from the one inhabited by Dyson and the lest. They were speaking a different tongue, there was a frontier drawn between them: he had strayed across into the picture and was as foreign as the rest of the components.

After the super had gone he phoned the Central Office, having to wait some minutes to get hold of Pagram. His associate sounded bored and he was drinking something while he talked.

'Take advice from me, old man ... the horse died years ago at this end. We've been flogging him like mad and he hasn't twitched a muscle. I think you can take it for granted that Campion was outside Mixer's rackets.'

'Have you got on to any of her ex's?'

'Yes, we've managed to contact two. One of them is an architect by the name of Lacey. The other keeps a junk shop at the right end of Fulham Road. Podmore, he's called, but no connection with the late chummy. Both of them clean and neither were near Hiverton. We've got another name, Coulson, but him we're still chasing.'

'What did they know about Campion?'

'Nothing, except that she buried her grand-mother. *Her* husband was a Charlie Campion, a foreman carpenter who hailed from Stepney. We dug that up at Somerset House, but there's no sign of any of their children having married. You can think what you like.'

'And the local records?'

'Gone up in smoke. But we're still asking questions.'

Gently inquired about the warehouse affair. Here everything was progress with arrests hourly expected. Mixer's associates had been identified as old friends of the police; there were men out searching for them in all their favoured localities.

'If only it wasn't so flaming hot! You've no idea what Whitehall's like.'

'Have you been frying any more eggs?'

'We tried some steak, but it just dries up.'

He lit his pipe and went into the bar. The news of the fresh discovery had quickly made its way to the guest house. At one or two of the tables they sat discussing it, but their voices sank as they saw him enter. Without looking round he knew that every head was turned.

'A shandy with plenty of ice.'

Maurice looked as though he wanted to speak to Gently. After making the drink he stood hesitating by the counter, put off by the silence and general focus of attention. But at last he leaned over and whispered in Gently's ear:

'Is it right what they're saying?'

Gently tilted his glass, shrugging. If that was all Maurice wanted, then he could wait for the evening paper. It wasn't all, however. The bartender remained with his elbows on the counter. His appearance was less confident than it had been in the morning and he watched the progress of the shandy with symptoms of anxiety.

'You remember what I was telling you?'

'Hmn.' Gently put down the glass.

'Well, I don't want you to think... I mean, I gave it to you straight! As near as I remember Rosie was in with me till one. If she says any different ... we didn't watch the clock, did we? I gave it to you straight, you needn't worry about that.'

Watching him, Gently grunted again. Maurice was noticeably more nervous, less inclined to be matey. It went without saying that he had compared notes with Rosie – had her memory been bad, and the truth leaked out by accident?

'What part of the world do you come from?'

'Me? I belong to Starmouth.'

'Your family lives there?'

'Well no – not exactly. But I've been settled up here for a few years now.'

'Where does your family live?'

'In Lambeth, as a matter of fact.'

'In Lambeth! When was the last time you were there?'

'To tell the truth, I haven't been home since after the war.'

The nervousness was alarm now – Maurice didn't like this at all. In spite of the ears cocked in their direction he was letting his voice rise from its confidential whisper.

'Look, I had some trouble, see? But it's all over and done with! I may as well admit it – it had to do with a woman. She swore I made her do it – you know how it is – tore her clothes and got some bruises! And all the time, if she'd told the truth.'

'How far is Lambeth from Camden Town?'

'I don't know! What's that got to do with it?'

'And how long did you say you'd known Miss Campion?'

'I told you – since last week. And the same goes with her boyfriend.'

'You'd better let me have your family's address.'

He left Maurice staring after him very unhappily. The bartender had the air of being completely taken down. He began polishing glasses which were sparkling bright already, and when he served a customer, kept his eyes strictly lowered.

'Pagram? It's me again. I've got another assignment for you.'

As he talked Gently could imagine the airless heat trap of the Lambeth streets.

Some of the youngsters had formed a skiffle group which practised in the reading room, and Gently, on his way out, caught a snatch from it in the hall. They weren't entirely beginners, you could tell it by their panache: just then they were improvising a rather neat calypso.

'Rachel, she was a lady –
At least, some people thought so!
Rachel, she was a lady –
At least, some people thought so!
Rachel came to the Bel-Air,
Rachel had long coal-black hair –
Rachel, she was all the rage,
Isn't it a pity she was in a cage!

Oh, we all liked Rachel so,
But not that other so-and-so!'

The performance ended in laughter and shrieks of applause. It was sung, Gently thought, by a certain fair-haired youth who played a good game of tennis. It depended on your age how you reacted to shock.

Did he have a premonition that he would find Esau waiting for him? He couldn't precisely have said, but at least the event didn't surprise him. The fisherman must have known that Gently would want to see him – no policeman was going to be satisfied by the events of that morning! At the same time, Esau didn't need to put himself forward; and that was what he was doing, sitting there on his hedge bank.

Or was he? Gently had to admit a second of doubt about it. The fisherman looked so unconcerned, his darkened clay resting between his teeth. He was, of course, ignoring Gently. The Sea-King paid his respects to no man. But surely he could be there for one purpose only, he wouldn't have chosen that seat by accident?

He was there, in any case, in his odd, inscrutable fashion. Gently advanced towards him deliberately, trying to frame his opening gambit. Then – instinctively – he wavered. What was the use in asking questions? Hadn't it already got beyond words with them, this majestic man and himself?

Instead, he sat down silently beside him. It seemed suddenly the only thing to be done. If there was to be any communication, then the initiative lay with Esau: Gently's role was to wait alertly for what the other might care to impart. They had got into a peculiar relationship and one could only give it its head.

And so it began, a bizarre half-hour, unequalled by anything in Gently's experience. Looking back on it from a distance he was still unable to make sense of it. Not a word was spoken by either, nor did they once exchange a look. If they had been a couple of statues they could hardly have sat stiller or quieter. Bizarre – and yet something did pass between them however inexplicable it was to remain. Gently became conscious of a growing clarity, a slow development of his earlier mood. Was the Sea-King a telepathist – could that be the explanation? Was he secretly shaping Gently's thoughts as the smoke rose from the guttering clay?

Perhaps it was simply the other's serenity which was being communicated to him. He sat so still, so effortlessly still, his eyes scarcely blinking or shifting direction. His face was as a mask from which all emotion had drained away: its lines contained a history, but of itself it had no expression. And sitting there beside him one had to echo that brooding serenity. It was like a sensible ether that he extended round about him. This it was, at the least, which was prompting Gently's awareness, soothing him, persuading him that he was seeing things more clearly.

Because, in sum, what was it that this clarity embraced? It was an indefinable conviction that now he knew all there was to be known. There was nothing material to support it, no new fact to square the circle. As intangible as the pipe smoke the conviction had stolen upon his mind. *Now* ... he knew it all! – Esau's silence was to tell him that. The facts were all before him, he needed only a moment of vision. Esau had done what he could for him. He had given him the hint that mattered. For the rest it was up to Gently to recognize the picture on the canvas.

Only here, unfortunately, his vision wouldn't carry. The very sharpness of the detail was perplexing his interpretation. The facts might well be there and he seeing them vividly, but as yet they wouldn't assemble into a revealing viewpoint.

Was he reading too much into his fascination with Esau – was he missing something simple but crucially important?

Twice their odd communion was broken by the passage of other people, and each time the interruption bore an interesting character. The first was when Maurice appeared on an errand into the village. On seeing them he drew back and seemed to debate whether he would continue. Eventually he did, though with some discomposure; he kept his eye on Gently as though he expected him to interfere.

The second intruder was Hawks, who was with them rather longer. It was apparent from a glance that they were his object in coming there. He came unsteadily up the road and stopped about twenty yards short of them; he remained for four or five minutes, staring hatred at one and the other.

A Hawks who had been drinking... But he contented himself with his stare. At the end of the session he lurched away again, probably to buy a last pint at The Longshoreman.

At this juncture Gently *did* risk a glance at Esau, but the Sea-King remained as unmoved as before. It was when Gently shrugged and felt for his pipe that the fisherman made his solitary gesture. Slowly, he picked up his pouch and offered it to the detective. The action was so unexpected that it seemed to carry a special point. Nothing else went with it, no nod, no inclination: just the extending of the pouch in the steady, gnarled hand.

Was it purely an accident that it happened when it did? Gently could never be certain, either then or afterwards. His reaching for his pipe had given Esau the opening – if he hadn't chanced to do so, what device would have been used?

The audience was ended peremptorily by the Sea-King getting to his feet. Gently, still in a state of bemusement, let him depart without demur. He was feeling again that uneasy reaction, that suspicion that perhaps the fisherman had fooled him. Oughtn't he to have cracked down hard on Esau – to have really put some pressure on him?

He grunted and tapped his pipe on his heel – twist had never been a favourite smoke with him. From the direction of the village he could see Maurice returning and with Maurice, at all events, he had no doubts about technique.

'Where have you just been?'

'Me? Down to the shop!'

'After what?'

'Well, if you're not going to be allowed to...'

Gently clicked his tongue in caustic admonishment.

'Come, come! Don't send me bothering the exchange. You've just been phoning Lambeth to let them know what's coming – and you thought it would be safer to do it in the village!'

The fact that he was right gave him a childish pleasure; it compensated his ego for the inroads made by Esau.

In the guest house trouble waited for him, wearing the face of Inspector Dyson. The County man had been talking to Stock and confirming his belief in Gently's duplicity. Gently fixed him with a drink and led him out on to the lawn. Dyson's face had reached the peeling stage: he was treating his arms as though they were made of glass.

'I'm afraid we still don't understand.'

He found it difficult to come to the point.

'The super thinks ... since you were on the other case. Mightn't there be a connection which perhaps, as yet...?'

That infernal connection! What in fact did it consist of? Contiguity was the one sure thing they had to go on. The sandhills body was much too old. It predated Simmonds and probably Rachel. Mixer had been a boy... Maurice a child... Hawks and Esau were the ones if they wanted to show connection. Esau, who had shown it to him, and Hawks, who kept getting drunk.

'Nothing further with missing persons?'

Dyson gloomily shook his head.

'I've been trying round the village – the postman, vicar – people like that. In a place as small as this you'd expect someone to remember. Everyone knows everybody. They couldn't disappear for a day. My own idea is that it was a visitor, but where do you start looking then?'

'A lot of visitors come from Norchester.'

'Yes, but there's nobody on their records. Then I had half a notion that it was someone from up here, but the super says you checked, and that as far as you know...'

It was true, Gently had seen the manager before lunch. The Bel-Air, like Hiverton, had a clean sheet of missing persons. They had phoned the manager's predecessor, who lived in retirement: the clean sheet extended to the Bel-Air's foundation.

'So we're left with a day tripper who didn't come from Norchester – raped and strangled, no doubt, though she might have been poisoned. And as the super points out...'

The parallel was rather striking: only one thing made a difference – that little matter of thirty years!

'Do you think it's just possible that we're after the same man?'

Gently could hardly keep a smile from straying over his face. Dyson was watching him like a cat, trying to surprise his guilty knowledge. For the Central Office man it was a unique experience.

'I don't see why not.'

'In that case, perhaps...?'

'I'm simply agreeing in principle. I don't say I know who did it.'

Yet didn't he, to be honest; wasn't he as certain as he could be? Hadn't Esau drawn up the case for him as plainly as in a written statement? It'd all happened before, that was the heart of the matter. Rachel's murder had been the echo of a crime in the past. Hawks had been a young man then, he'd been tall, athletic, handsome. The bitter sourness of his face was something still to be contracted.

An Adonis, keen on women! And unlike Maurice, with taking qualities. In the wreck of the man one could see what he had been, one could glimpse the bright flame that tragedy had dimmed. And Esau, he knew what had wrought that change. They had been mates together ... brothers ... fishermen. He had known of the passionate crime which took place in the marrams, but it was a fisherman's crime and his mouth was closed.

And the years had passed over it, but they hadn't washed it clean. The secret had raised a barrier between the two men. It tied them together but also it held them apart: they were married, one to the other, in a fearsome, life-long alliance. And it had set its stamp on them according to their natures. Hawks it had made savage, Esau a solitary. Unacknowledged, unshriven, it had worked its deadly ends; one of them had sunk beneath it and the other found a lonely eminence.

Then Rachel had come with her devastating beauty: Rachel, stirring passions which had slept for thirty years. Had Esau seen it happening, seen the madness begin to gather? Had he tried to watch over her and to prevent the second outbreak?

Yes, at the bottom of him Gently knew it: *this* was the case which Esau had sketched for him. The fisherman had eased his conscience of the burden which lay on it and done it without providing one atom of proof! How could one broach such a matter to the sharp-eyed, rational Dyson?

'If you say so, of course, then we're bound to take your word. But it seemed a bit peculiar, you just finding it like that.'

'I noticed the shape of that clump. You can put down the rest to a suspicious nature.'

'And there's positively no link-up?'

'Nothing one could prove in court.'

'Still, a lead of any sort...'

Gently sighed and mopped his brow. He couldn't very well tell Dyson to stop interfering! The man was doing his duty in spite of the heat and a dose of sunburn. A little professional co-operation wasn't too much to be expected.

'If anything turns up, I promise you faithfully ... at the moment, I could put Simmonds in the dock. I've got a hunch, but it may be no more. Just now I'm rather keen to know the identity of those bones.'

Dyson nodded resignedly. 'Nineteen-thirty's so long ago.'

'Nineteen-thirty?'

'Didn't I tell you? We've had an expert on the shoes.'

Gently had another question but he was prevented from putting it. Maurice came up, sulky faced, with a scribbled note from Dutt.

'Says to tell you it was urgent – there's a

bloke going to jump off the church tower.'

The note was more explicit. The bloke in question was John Peter Simmonds.

CHAPTER ELEVEN

'That bloody little fool!'

Gently kept on repeating it: the words seemed to put the situation in a nutshell. Since ten o'clock that morning he'd almost forgotten the artist's existence; he hadn't wanted to think about Simmonds at all. He'd found a different angle, one a good deal more intriguing. Now, he knew, he'd let it dominate him, let it thrust Simmonds out of his reckoning.

'It looks as though you were right.'

'That bloody little fool!'

'If you can manage to get him down...'

'I should have locked him up yesterday!'

It was impossible to drive fast because of the helter-skelter of people. From all directions they were running and scurrying towards the churchyard. Shopkeepers, housewives, visitors, fishermen, they paid no attention to the Wolseley's blaring horn.

'That bloody little fool!'

Was it his conscience that kept repeating it? If Dyson had said much to him he'd have jumped down the man's throat. And really he was blaming Esau; Esau who had laid the spell on him. For several hours now he'd been living in a kind of dream.

He slammed the Wolseley on to the verge about a hundred yards from the church. The crowd spread out ahead of him made it pointless to drive further. One caught sight of the artist directly: he had got out on a ledge below the parapet. His white face made a splodge against the dark grey of the flint and his hands, apparently bleeding, were grasping at the rough, sharp-edged stones.

Beneath him everything was in an uproar – the crowd were excited and partly hysterical. Leaving an ominous half-circle at the foot of the tower, they were shoving and pushing together in the churchyard and the road. They scarcely noticed Gently as he shouldered his way through them. They had eyes and thoughts for only one object.

'Do you really think he'll do it?'

'If you were going to be hung!'

And from a slattern carrying a baby: 'Why doesn't he get on with it?'

All of Hiverton had collected there or were

on the point of arriving. Some were still wearing aprons or carrying tokens of their occupation. In the forefront of the half-circle were stationed the reporters and the cameramen; the latter were studying angles and pointing to the withered turf in front of them.

'It's no good sir – he won't come down.'

Dutt came struggling through the crowd, his streaming face plastered over with grime.

'I've been shouting to him from the belfry. He won't take a bit of notice. I'm sorry, sir, but he did me. I let him go in the church by himself.'

'Can't we get on the tower and grab him?'

'No sir. He's fixed the blinking trap door. There's only a ladder goes up to it, and he's piled something heavy on top.'

'The stones ... there were some stones left up there.'

Jack Spanton, standing near them, volunteered the information.

'They were repairing the tower – Sam Nickerson told me. They left the stones up there ... too lazy to bring them down!'

'What about some ladders?'

'Mears is fetching one from the vicarage.'

'One! How high do you reckon he is?'

'According to the vicar, a hundred and thirty...'

Gently twisted on his heel without waiting for Dutt to finish. Across the road, on the verge, he could see a reporter in a phone box. It was the man on the *Echo*, and he hurriedly fed in some coins: it didn't do any good – he was yanked out with small ceremony.

'Starmouth Fire Services – quick!'

He turned his back on the indignant reporter. Through the glass panels of the box he caught a momentary glimpse of Hawks. The fellow was standing behind the others where he thought he was unobserved; his face was a picture of gloating triumph, his eyes seemed to devour the clinging figure.

'Chief Inspector Gently. I want an expanding ladder at Hiverton.'

The fire officer listened carefully as the situation was described to him.

'But a hundred feet's our limit ... there's nothing higher this side of London.'

'Then send me out a catching net.'

'From that height, he'd probably go straight through it.'

Outside a silence had fallen: the crowd was stilled, intent and listening. Simmonds was shouting something down to them, his girlish voice sounding thin with hysteria. Gently kicked open the phone-box door and held it ajar with a prodding sandal.

'You can't get at me now... I'm out of your power. Hang someone else ... you'll never hang me! Hang someone else!'

At that point they obviously thought he was going to do it. They shuffled and crowded away from the tower. The photographers, combining for maximum coverage, had trained their cameras at three different angles. One would catch him jumping, one falling, one striking: the latter had a reporter by him to give him a slap on the shoulder.

But Simmonds didn't jump, he remained transfixed against the tower. His bloody hands, spread out each side, still fumbled and clutched at the sun-hot flint. The crowd gave a sigh and a reporter swore:

'We'll lose the last editions if he doesn't make his mind up!'

Now there was a stir from another quarter – Mears and the vicar were bringing a ladder. For some reason nobody thought of its pitiful inadequacy: it was a ladder, a symbol, a token of something being done. Unhesitatingly they fell back to let the two men come through. Mears, in a fury of blind intention, set it wavering against the tower. Then he climbed it – twenty-five feet – and stood panting on the top-most rungs; for an instant, by sheer suggestion, a rescue seemed not entirely impossible.

'Starmouth! Are you still there?'

'Sorry. I thought you must have rung off.'

'Send anything you like – I don't care what! Just send it quickly or you'll be too late.'

'Roger – but you might as well know in advance...'

He buttonholed Dutt, who was standing by helplessly. Dyson he'd lost sight of as soon as they'd parked the car.

'Show me the way up. I'm going to have a talk with him. And I want to see that trap door, just in case there's a way...'

The interior of the church was cool and very gloomy, appearing quite dark after the glare without. Their feet rang echoingly on uncovered tiles, there was an odour of oil lamps and slightly-damp plaster. A door with a pointed top gave them access to the stairway. It was a narrow brick spiral, its sagging steps lit only occasionally.

'Here you are, sir ... the belfry.'

Gently came out gasping for breath. All around him hung dim shapes, leaving scarcely room to stand upright. Hiverton, apparently, had a peal, a little fortune in bell metal. Five of them hung cheek-by-jowl, but the sixth – Gently stepped back hastily.

'My God – there's one of them swung!

Didn't you notice it when you were up here?'

The largest bell of all was pointing its mouth towards the ceiling. A couple of tons at least, it rested poised like a juggler's bowl: a gentle touch, a sudden vibration, and down it would sweep, crushing all in its path.

'We'll have to let it be – the noise might make him lose his balance. Just keep over there, that's all ... and say some prayers as I go up the ladder!'

But he knew the trap door was out, with that bell yawning there beside it. There could be no attack with a crowbar unless one was prepared to be swiped into oblivion. He climbed up gingerly and tried the door. It felt as firm as the walls round about it. Furthermore, one daren't exert any pressure, since the rungs of the ladder were ancient and worm-eaten.

'Where were you when you shouted to him?'

'Up there, sir, where you are now.'

'This bell ... didn't it even occur to you?'

'Bells are a little bit out of my line, sir.'

Gently shivered and made his way down again – he had nearly lost himself a sergeant! And Simmonds, though he wouldn't appreciate it, was probably lucky still to be alive. But he had burned his boats, the artist. There was no coming at him from within or without. If that was what he'd wanted then he'd done it with a vengeance … he was out of their power: the bloody little fool!

To disseminate its chimes the belfry had four slatted windows. Gently moved across to the one above which he knew the artist was clinging. Through the slats he could see the scene below him, the patient semi-circle of up-turned faces. Another reporter had taken possession of the phone box, and Mears, giving it up, was climbing disconsolately down his ladder.

'Simmonds … can you hear me?'

He didn't dare to raise his voice. The thought of that bell behind him was choking back the words in his throat. 'Simmonds, listen to me! Stop making an exhibition out there. Can't you see you're playing to them … can't you see them waiting there with their cameras?'

From the crowd came a whispering murmur, rather like the stirring of leaves. Something was clearly taking place upon the ledge just over his head. He jammed his face against the slats, but at the angle it was impossible to see anything. At the best he could hear a faint sound that suggested the scraping of a shoe.

'Get back on the roof, Simmonds – we'll get you away, I promise you that! There'll be no more photographers – we'll keep you here till after dark. They won't get another look in. We'll drive you straight back to Norchester. Are you listening to me, Simmonds ... can you hear what I say?'

He kept his eyes fixed on the crowd, trying to interpret their reactions. They must surely let him know if the artist made a definite move! But the murmur had died away and a head or two was turning. Whatever he had done was over now, he must have resumed his original posture.

'Simmonds ... I know you can hear me!'

Again that slight scraping and a ripple from the crowd.

'Don't give them what they want – you're letting them drive you into it. Get back on the roof and let them see that you despise them!'

'It's too late ... too late for that.'

He caught his breath at the sound of the voice. Simmonds was closer than he expected – was he bending down to Gently?

'Don't you understand? They've finished me.'

'Nonsense! Get back on the roof.'

'No ... I'm finished ... they've murdered

me! If you want to hang someone ... why not *them?*'

The ripple of the crowd had increased to a buzzing. They couldn't understand what it was that was going on. An alert reporter was stealing quietly towards the church door: Gently made a dumbshow to Dutt, who disappeared down the stairway.

'You're taking it the wrong way, Simmonds! Can't we talk it over?'

'It's too late, I tell you ... there's nothing else left.'

'Would you have acted like this if your mother had been alive?'

'Don't talk about her! You'd never understand.'

'She'd have expected better of you.'

'Please ... don't talk about her.'

Yes, he must be stooping somehow, on his bare six inches of ledge. Gently could see the image of it reflected in several hundred pairs of eyes. He had moved along, and stooped – had he then such a clear head for heights? As though to confirm the guess, one of the photographers took a fresh shot.

'Can't you see what it is they've done? My life ... it's been taken away! I can't ever go back again ... they've destroyed everything that I was. It doesn't matter if I'm guilty or not. All the same, they've finished me off!'

'And you're going to let them do it?'

'It's done ... it's no use pretending.'

'There's your art. Are you forgetting that?'

'They've got that too ... everything, they've taken!'

'No.' Gently shook his head from habit. 'That's one thing they can't take. The rest, perhaps, you'll have to begin again, but nothing can make you other than a painter. *There* you've got them beaten before they start.'

'I tell you they've killed me. I can never paint again.'

'That's what you think now.'

'It's true. I'm done for!'

'You are, if you're not going to give yourself a chance.'

Gently hung on a moment, uncertain of what he was going to say. He had never been much of a hand at a sermon. For the best part of one's life one was dealing with trivia, and then, when the need arose ... was it the contact he needed?

'Take a week, take a month, take a year to think it over. There's plenty of time when it comes to dying. They may have killed something, but that isn't important. It's only the past that's done for: there's always the future.'

'There isn't any future.'

'Yes there is. It's always there. And there's always part of us dying to make room for what's coming along.'

'But not in this way.'

'In this or another. Did you want to stay put, and be exactly as you were?'

'You're twisting it ... making it seem...'

'I'm telling the truth, and you know it.'

'It doesn't apply!'

'It applies to all the world.'

If he could only see what was going on above him! The voice, by itself, didn't tell him what he wanted to know. Down below they were quite still, sensing that something was in the balance. From the direction of the stairway he could hear Dutt's voice in altercation.

'Are you still listening to me, Simmonds?'

At all events, he must keep him talking. Every minute he could gain was swinging the chance in his direction.

'Do you think it will bring her back, your doing a silly thing like this? Is throwing yourself off there going to prove that you were innocent?'

'I don't care about that now!'

'Not that someone murdered Rachel?'

'It doesn't matter any more ... everyone

knows that it was me.'

'They don't know anything of the sort.'

'Oh yes they do! You, and the rest. It's no good saying anything. I'm the one they want to hang.'

'Listen to me, Simmonds!'

'No ... I'm tired of listening...'

'I'm the one who counts, not that pack of wolves down there. And I haven't charged you, have I? I haven't even put it to you! At the moment you're simply a material witness, and I don't expect that you'll be anything else. So why not stop playing up to them and come back inside?'

'I've told you ... I don't care.'

'You do, and you're going to show it.'

'They can think what they like – only let me alone! I don't want to talk and I'm tired of listening.'

A movement below him warned Gently that he was losing. The photographers, who had relaxed, now froze again behind their cameras. The one lens was staring towards him like a petrified eye, one was slightly tilted, one riveted upon the turf ... and once more, from overhead, came the sound of a scraping shoe.

'Simmonds!'

He felt the panic racing in his veins.

225

'*Simmonds!*'

'Go away. I won't listen any more.'

Suddenly the scraping became a scrabbling noise, violent and desperate: the sound of a foot searching madly for a hold. The up-turned faces swayed as though caught by a wind, some were being hidden, some twisted away. And then – it stopped, that scrabbling. The foot had found its hold. And a groan drifted up like the moaning of the sea.

'Simmonds!'

Gently found himself whispering it too softly to be heard. He didn't need telling that he had lost in that encounter. Simmonds had heard what he could say, and he daren't say any more: now, a repetition of it might be hastening the end. At least the artist had struggled when he felt himself beginning to slip.

'I've locked the door down there, sir.'

Dutt toiled wearily out of the stairway.

'They was making a fuss about the church being public, but I barged them outside and turned the key pretty quick. I reckoned it wasn't public, sir, unless we said so.'

Gently shrugged, passing a dirty hand over his face. He could still hear the scuffling of that fear-stricken foot. Would he have watched as Simmonds's body went plunging past him ... would he have held to his post during the next few seconds?

'The Fire Service – why the devil isn't it here?'

Dutt echoed the shrug. 'Will it be any use, sir?'

'That isn't the point – it ought to be here! Isn't it part of their job to handle a business of this kind?'

He went stumping down the stairs in a blaze of irrational anger. Twenty minutes had passed and no fire engine arrived! But at heart he knew it was because he would never have watched that fall ... and because, in turning away from it, he would have in some way felt traitorous.

Towards whom? Towards what? – he didn't want to understand! There was nothing to be done except to be angry with the Fire Service.

Under the tower a fresh enterprise had engaged the crowd's attention. The vicar was ascending the ladder, presumably with the object of addressing Simmonds. He was a neat, smallish man who carried his three-score years with a flourish; he had short grey hair and a pallid, boyish face. He made no bones at all about frisking up the ladder.

'Young man up there!'

His voice was clear, and ringing. Even hanging on to a ladder he preserved an air of clerical dignity.

'Young man, are you aware of the gravity of your behaviour? Are you aware of the awful sin you are about to commit before the eyes of God?'

Simmonds was perched exactly where Gently had first seen him, a little to the left of the belfry window. There could be no doubt that he had shuffled along the ledge and perilously knelt for that abortive interview.

'Young man, I am praying for you, I am praying for your enlightenment. May God, in His infinite mercy, remove the cloud from your understanding. He it was Who gave you life, not, as you presume, to be wilfully disposed of.'

Was he listening, pressed to the stones, the blood now drying on his restless hands?

Hawks, Gently saw, had edged a yard or two closer, his expression changed to one of indignant anxiety. His dark eyes were boring into the figure of the artist, he seemed to be willing him to make the fatal decision.

'Dare you face your Creator, young man, in such sin? Will you meet Him this day with such a burden of guilt?'

A little girl began to cry and was snatched

up by her mother: a man, looking pale, seated himself upon a tombstone.

'I beseech you to think again – think of those who hold you dearly.'

If Simmonds would just keep still with those Cain-like hands.

'Your life is a precious thing, redeemed for you by Christ Jesu: put your trust in the Lord and preserve your immortal soul!'

The vicar had done and was bowing his head in prayer. Several of those round about had their hats in their hands. In all it was like a sacrament, a last rite for the dying; all earthly aid had been rendered, only the event now remained. And Simmonds ... his hands were stiffening, they were pressing him out into the void: he was balancing on the edge only a hairbreath from eternity.

'No!'

The stifled cry coming from him scarcely seemed a human utterance. It was wrenched from between teeth set together like a trap.

'I don't want to die. Oh God, I don't want to! Get me down off here ... get me ... get me down!'

He was back against the wall, scooping at it in a frenzy. For the first time he seemed to understand his frightful position. He cringed against the flint, his knees sagging, his body trembling: they could hear his breath coming in little suffocated gasps.

'Someone get me down!'

His face was ghastly with its terror. Nothing remained of the insensate coolness which till now had carried him along.

'I don't want to die ... help me ... come and get me down!'

In a moment or two, it seemed, he must slither off the ledge.

And nobody could do a thing! They would liked to have done, now. The whole current of the affair had undergone a change. Simmonds was no longer braving them, flouting them, indicting them: with his terror and his cries he was back on their side.

'Simmonds ... get back on the roof.'

'Get back – get back!'

Gently's shout was repeated by a hundred different voices. 'Reach up to the parapet – pull yourself over!'

'Put your foot on the spout!'

'Just heave and roll over!'

Sobbing and panting the artist made a feeble effort, but in doing so he nearly lost his balance on the ledge. He screamed like a child and fell back into a crouch. A piece of rubble fell pattering among the reporters.

'Can't we get up inside?'

There was a panic to be doing something. Two fishermen wanted to run for their nets. Remembering the bell, Gently sent Dutt to guard the church door. Dyson had popped up in the phone box where he was bawling unintelligibly to someone.

'Get me down ... get me down!'

Simmonds's voice had sunk to a wail, and the quality of death itself was echoing in that plea. He couldn't last for very much longer – you could hear it in every vibration. Like a dislodged sack of flour he was going to slither from his perch.

'Sir – come here a minute!'

Dutt was beckoning to him from the doorway.

'According to the bloke what keeps the pub, that fisherman has just gone into the church.'

'Fisherman? Which one is that?'

'The big bloke – Dawes, I think they call him.'

'Dawes! Has he gone up into the tower?'

'I reckon so, sir. He isn't inside.'

Esau ... gone up into the tower! Gently stared at the sergeant in amazement. What was the Sea-King doing up there, that silent, unpredictable man of mystery?

'Hadn't I better fetch him down, sir?'

'Yes ... but watch your step in the belfry. If he gives you any trouble I'll send Mears to lend a hand.'

Just then the crowd gave a shout and made him turn in apprehension, but the artist still crouched on the ledge, still clung to his last few moments of life. It was something else that was happening up there! – The slats of the window were being driven outwards. Through the disintegrating wood came a jabbing sea boot, thrusting, splintering, and smashing at the framework.

'It's Esau ... he's going to get him!'

Was it physical, that surge of hope? There was a roar in their throats like the roar of a football crowd, unconscious, compulsive, a single, primitive voice. The Sea-King would do something – he was more than mere humanity! He could grapple with the impossible, he could wrest it to a conclusion.

Through the fragments came the fisherman with majestic unconcern. He might have been drawing himself through a hedge, so little concern did he seem to attach to it. Having got through the window he reached up for the ledge, and having grasped that, rose easily on to it As a feat of strength it was fantastic, it could have baffled a trained gymnast: yet the white-bearded giant made it seem a matter of course. With a quiet word to Simmonds he went up and over the parapet, then, taking the artist by his armpits, he drew him firmly on to the roof.

Pandemonium broke loose! It was the only word to describe it. Gently himself was babbling something, he could never remember what. The uproar was so deafening that one never noticed the fire engine – its crew must have thought that they'd stumbled into bedlam. Some were running into the church, some embracing each other: even the reporters were shaking hands and dancing about like the rest. Above the tumult the sudden tolling of the bell sounded quite in order – it had to clang three times before Gently realized...

But, after all, he needn't have worried. Nothing, it appeared was to spoil that moment. The bell had deafened poor Dutt – he was deaf for a week – but it had done nothing else except to stir up dust. Gently arrived just in time to see the trap door opening. He helped to bring the collapsing artist down the rickety ladder. Esau, always Esau, was slowly piling the stones in a heap; he wouldn't even look at Gently, wouldn't answer a word that was put to him.

'Nothing but shock, is it?'

Dyson had forced the Wolseley through to the gate. From porch to road it might well have been a wedding – everyone was trying to pat Simmonds on the back.

'The shock – but that's enough!'

Simmonds was only partly conscious. His feet were dragging after him and he needed support on both sides.

'To the Police House, then?'

'Yes – and get a doctor to him. Take Mears along with you. His wife'll know what to do.'

The crowd hadn't time to take it in before the artist was whisked away. The reporters, too, were rather at a loss. But then they remembered Esau – Esau, who had worked the miracle. Could it be that he'd escaped in the excitement surrounding Simmonds?

No, Esau was there – at least, for their cameras. Gently could have told them not to expect more than that. The Sea-King came out of the church with his admirers crowding about him ... at a distance, a little distance: he had the divinity that hedges kings.

'Dawes is the name, isn't it?'

'Were you born in the village?'

Did they really think he was going to answer their pitiful stock of questions? He paid no more regard to them than to the fluttering black flies – perhaps a little less, because the flies told him something.

'There's a storm coming up.'

To himself he murmured it. They were the only words that Gently had heard pass his lips that day. A storm was coming up! – he turned his steps towards the beach. The reporters, still to learn wisdom, hurried after him in a pack.

But the drama wasn't quite finished under that lowering, blind-eyed tower. By the gate was standing Hawks with a look of murder on his face. He waited till Esau drew level, then he spat, full at the other: all the hate in his warped being was concentrated in the action. Esau's arm swept in a gesture, as though he brushed away an insect. Hawks went rolling in the dust. There was no more to it than that.

CHAPTER TWELVE

For a long time Gently stood still beside the spot where Hawks had fallen. The fisherman had scrambled to his feet and gone off after the others. A good few of the crowd still remained there, talking, and the vicar was turning some small boys out of the churchyard. Dutt had accompanied Simmonds – he still felt responsible for him, and Mears, who had returned the ladder, was now pedalling off on his cycle.

It was over – it was calming down; things were getting back to normal. Why, then, did he have this feeling that in reality they had just begun? Something had clicked as he saw Hawks go sprawling in the road, a premonition, an unconscious warning, you could call it what you liked. A climax was being reached: he couldn't get any closer to it. A climax of a tragic nature, coming up like the storm. Yet what, excepting imagination, was suggesting this present catastrophe? What harm could come to the Sea-King, with his rout of subjects about him?

He stood a long time, vacillating! His instinct was to follow Esau. His whole being seemed to pulse with a blind necessity for it. Against that there was feeble reason and some questions he had for the vicar: Dyson, no doubt, had asked the wrong ones, or he hadn't known what to ask.

It was the vicar who finally settled him, coming over to Gently voluntarily. Would the inspector step across the road for a glass of home-made lemonade? Gently went, though with grave misgivings. He couldn't conquer his foreboding so easily. But there were no rational grounds for it and the vicar was on the spot ... what else could he do but seize time by the forelock?

The vicar was a widower who lived with his youngest daughter. She was a plain-faced but smiling girl of two- or three-and-twenty. The vicarage was a large one and bore affinities to the Bel-Air; it was sparsely furnished with old, worn furniture, and yet, all the same, had an air of negligent comfort.

'A terrible, terrible business, Inspector.'

The vicar had taken him into what was obviously his den. A roll-top desk occupied a space by the window and the other three walls were lined with bookshelves. The books themselves were cheerfully dilapidated. Quite a number of them were innocent of backstrips and covers. The desk was littered with papers, some of them weighted with lumps of amber. Above the desk, in a frame of maple wood, hung a photograph of a college eight.

'That poor young man! What in the world constrained him to do it? Upon my word, it was a mercy that Skipper Dawes...'

Gently shrugged and looked for an ashtray in which to scrape out his pipe. Had the vicar called him in to see what he could

pump from him? Soon the daughter reappeared carrying the lemonade on a tray.
While he poured it the vicar continued his
musings and exclamations.

'In your business, Inspector...'

'We don't see a lot of suicide.'

'But to a certain extent you must be in-
ured to these things. I understand that the
young man...'

'He is a material witness.'

'I had heard, perhaps, incorrectly...'

'There's always gossip in these cases.'

The vicar nodded his head gravely. It was
probably wrong to suspect him. He was
shocked by what had happened and wanted
to talk it over with someone.

'I feel that if ever prayer was answered...'

'You did more for him than I did.'

'You, too, have the conviction?'

'Didn't you make him change his mind?'

He was afraid he had earned a lecture by
this hint of unbelief. Over his tumbler of
lemonade the vicar was staring at him
solemnly. Then he sighed, and took a pull
from it. This wasn't, perhaps, the time!
Gently, poker-faced behind his pipe, looked
less than apt as a subject for lectures.

'I had a visit from your colleague.'

'Yes.' Gently puffed a ring of smoke.

'I couldn't help him much, I'm afraid, unless it was help of a negative nature. These have been truly distressing days, Inspector. We live in an atmosphere of doubt. The sin of one man can infect a community – in a sense, we are all of us sharers in his guilt.'

'You are referring to society?'

'Every one of us, Inspector. The commission of a crime is like a ripple in a pond. We have impulses of good and impulses of evil, and both can be excited by the presence of their like. Those people out there! They are good souls, all of them. Many of them I have known all the days of their lives. Yet in the presence of sin they become themselves sinful, they feel guilt in themselves and their hearts become as stone. When you find your culprit and bring him to the gallows their guilt, I'm afraid, not their justice, will rejoice.

'The most tragic two words in the language are "Crucify him!" There, Inspector, lies the shipwreck of the human spirit.'

Gently nodded without comment – he hadn't come to discuss the morals of it. At the moment he wanted something more directly germane. 'All the days of their lives' was the phrase which had struck him ... the vicar was an observer who might hold vital information.

'How long have you been in Hiverton?'

'Don't ask me, Inspector!'

He pointed to his short grey hair with a smile.

'I came here from Tuthill – that's a parish in Dorset. It was winter at the time and I thought I'd come to the North Pole.'

'Many years ago, was it?'

'In twenty-seven, to be exact. I ought to remember it because poor Mary was having John. We were snowed up for three weeks – no hope of a midwife. John was our first, you know. I shall never forget it.'

'Things have changed, I expect.'

'Yes. Even in Hiverton.'

'And people, no doubt.'

'They change, but they stay the same.'

'The fishermen too?'

'Especially the fishermen! They haven't altered, Inspector, since Peter cast his nets in Galilee.'

'What about Robert Hawks?'

'Are you interested in Bob?'

'I'd like to hear anything you can tell me about him.'

The vicar, rather to Gently's surprise, himself produced a pipe. It was a pleasant little briar with an apple-shaped bowl. He tapped it once or twice fastidiously before filling it from a tin – the mixture, Gently noticed, was a mild-flavoured blend.

'You've been using your eyes, haven't you?'

Gently offered his matches, shrugging. The vicar lit his pipe attentively, letting the match burn almost to his fingers.

'In fact, it wouldn't surprise me ... how much do you really know about them? Because Dawes comes into it, all along the line. If you're interested in one then you're interested in the other.'

'In both if you like. I was going to ask about Esau.'

The vicar nodded wisely and adjusted his pipe with his thumb.

'Well, when I first came here, things were altogether different. In those days they used to go drifting – Esau's got his skipper's ticket. As a matter of fact, I didn't see much of them. They used to follow the fishing for the best part of the year, and were at Hiverton for only a few weeks at a time.'

'How long did that continue?'

'Oh, only for a year or two. I imagine they were saving their money to buy themselves boats. But what I was going to tell you was that then they were the best of friends – now, as you may have seen, they're on a rather peculiar footing.

241

'Bob, when I first knew him, would be round about thirty. He was a swashbuckling young man with very good looks. You've seen those dark eyes of his – they played havoc among the females. And he was a spark in those days, he'd got a joke for everyone.

'Esau was a few years older and a steadier type altogether. He was always a bit reserved, a bit distant from the other fishermen. He was a skipper, which made a difference. He got his ticket very young. I believe he was very much sought after and had a wonderful record of catches.

'Well then, as I say, they bought themselves boats – or more likely, Esau bought them: he was the one to have had the money. Esau's boat was built at Wrackstead. I can remember them bringing it round. It's unique in the line of fishing boats and there were pictures of it in the *Eastern Daily Post*.'

'Can you remember what year that was?'

'It was the spring of twenty-nine. Mary was having Anne, and she was born on the first of June.'

'How did they get on with the boats?'

'Oh, well – at least, Esau did. Bob, I imagine, was paying off instalments, but I don't think it was that which came in between them. Esau had a spanking year. He was after his second boat. He owned five altogether by thirty-two or three, and later, for no good reason, he sold them off again. You'll have to do a lot of probing, Inspector, to get to the bottom of Esau.'

'But this thing … whatever it was?'

'That's just what I'm coming to now.'

The vicar re-lit his pipe with a little conscious art; but then, after puffing once or twice, he produced an anticlimax.

'I don't know what caused it, and that's being honest with you. I can't even be sure of when it took place. They're chapel, you know, like most of the fishermen, and not so close to me as my own congregation. But – something went wrong, that was plain to everyone. You never saw them together again as they were in the old days. Esau shut himself up just the way he is now and Bob – well, you've seen him. He changed out of mind.

'But this is the odd thing, and I could never make it out. Esau gained a remarkable ascendancy over Bob. It seemed that the further they drifted apart, the more Bob stood in awe of him; whenever he was by poor Bob became as quiet as a lamb.

'Esau, you can guess, had always been the dominant partner, and Bob wasn't the only one to feel himself subjected. You must have noticed Esau's standing. He's a sort of high priest to the fishermen. He's got more authority than I have with them, and I'm bound to admit that he uses it wisely.

'But that doesn't account for his ascendancy over Bob. There you've got something quite out of the natural order. I'm certain that Bob hates him – bless me for saying so! – yet he goes in perpetual subjugation to the man.'

'And you've nothing to suggest?'

'I haven't, Inspector. This is Hiverton's mystery and has been for years. If you're thinking of solving it, then I give you fair warning. I've lived half my life with it and have never had an inkling.'

He puffed away complacently, his pale hands on his knees. He was obviously enjoying this chat about his parishioners. It was getting Gently nowhere, except to confirm his guesses. All that the priest had told him so far was only corroborating the Sea-King.

Gently was party to Hiverton's mystery, but the proof was still out of his hands!

'You say you couldn't be sure when it happened?'

'No ... if you want me to be exact. It's the negative sort of thing that one doesn't at first notice. It might go on for years before your attention gets drawn to it.'

'What drew your attention to it?'

'Some gossip, I dare say. Like every other village, Hiverton is well served in that line.'

'It was before the war, of course?'

'Oh yes, a good while before. If you're pinning me down I would say the early thirties – but don't rely on my memory too much.'

'Just after they bought the boats?'

'Yes, it wouldn't have been so long after. But I've long given up the view that money had anything to do with it. They'd have ironed out their money troubles and have forgotten them by now. Bob, you must understand, has never been unprosperous.'

'He never married, did he?'

'No, and that again was peculiar. He used to be fond of the girls, and then he was all the other way.'

'Dating from this trouble between them?'

'More or less, now you come to mention it.'

'Didn't that ever strike you as significant?'

'Not before ... and I can't see it now.'

Still it was only corroborative, though the corroboration was growing stronger. Touch it where you would and it gave you solid support for Esau. And surely the proof must come, if one could frame the definitive question – the revealing answer was there, it needed only to be evoked!

'Did he have any trouble with women?'

'I believe so. From time to time.'

'Anything special that you can remember?'

'Yes ... there was scandal about one girl. Her name was Platten, I seem to recall ... she was engaged to a fellow at Hamby. Her first child was born rather soon after the wedding and rumour had it that her husband thrashed Robert.'

'What happened to her afterwards?'

'She's still living in Hamby. Her husband keeps the Marquis and her daughter married a Gorbold.'

'And she's the child in question?'

'No, that was a "he". They christened him Japheth – he's in the Merchant Navy.'

The vicar gave a little chuckle as though something amusing had struck him. He tapped his pipe on his palm and looked at Gently with a quizzical twinkle.

'You haven't asked about Esau. Doesn't he impress you as being marriageable?'

'Esau!'

'Yes – I thought you'd stare! But I assure you that he's a married man.'

Gently sat very still, his pipe rigid between his teeth. For a second or two he was unable to speak a word. The vicar smiled broadly at the impression he had made – here was something that had astonished the un-astonishable chief inspector!

'You're quite certain, about this?'

'My dear fellow, I married him. It was a particular triumph since he was such a stout chapelite. His lady, I'm afraid, had no convictions either way, but I imagine that she felt the church would give a better tone to the occasion.'

'And his wife – *where is she?*'

'He kicked her out, years ago. They were an ill-assorted couple, Esau and his Josephine. She was a foreigner, you know – that's to say, she wasn't Northshire. I could have told the skipper he was making a mistake, though, of course, he didn't ask my advice.'

Gently could only shake his head. The information had struck him like a bludgeon. Almost anything but this he had been preparing himself to hear. It was nudging the whole foundation, the very groundworks of the case – in a moment, he could sense, the structure would crash about his ears.

'Where did she come from?'

'Josephine?'

'From Camden Town, by any chance?'

'She certainly came from London, though I don't recall what part. Esau met her on a

247

fishing trip – it was when he was on the drifters. I have a hazy impression that they met in Ramsgate or Margate.'

'What was her name?'

'That's asking too much! But if you want to know we can find it in the register.'

'Can you remember the year she left him?'

'Precisely. It was in the summer of nineteen-thirty.'

He was aware of the vicar staring at him gravely, a puckered little frown on the ecclesiastical brow. He had laid his pipe aside and placed the tips of his fingers together: now he was rocking them towards Gently in a manner of gentle reproof.

'I'm not an idiot, you know, and I can guess what's in your mind. Your colleague has already told me about that skeleton in the marrams But it won't do, Inspector, it won't do at all. There's a couple of hundred witnesses that Mrs Dawes really left her husband.'

'A couple of hundred witnesses!'

Gently couldn't help his incredulity.

'A couple of hundred or *more,* and I was one of them myself. It was a seven-day wonder at Hiverton. The village talked about it for weeks. She went off to the station in Albert Johnson's hire car, swearing like a trooper and cursing Esau to high heaven. It was a tragedy, I admit, but not the sort that you're thinking of.'

'That was the last that was heard of her?'

'You're wrong again. She wrote to her acquaintances. Our maid at the time had a letter from Josephine – it was a shocking epistle, highly ungrammatical.'

'You saw it, did you?'

'I did, Inspector. It made me congratulate myself on being rid of such a parishioner. After applying every conceivable epithet to her husband she declared her intention of never again leaving London. And she never did, you can be certain. There has never been a whisper of her. She couldn't have set foot here without the whole village buzzing of it.'

'And that was in the summer of nineteen-thirty?'

'Yes, almost a year from the day on which I married them.'

'Was there a child of the marriage?'

'It was unblessed in every way.'

'If you've no objections I should like to use your phone.'

The phone was in a niche under the stairs in the hall, and to use it one was obliged to adopt a semi-crouched position. As always there was a wait before Pagram came on: for

249

what seemed like half-an-hour he was listening to the exchange's murmur.

'Pagram? Listen carefully – there've been further developments. It's Campion's mother that I want you to get a line on. Her name may be Dawes, a Mrs Esau Dawes; and she may have been living with her mother in the summer of nineteen-thirty. The vital thing to know...'

He heard Pagram's delighted chuckle.

'This time we've beaten you to the punch, old horse! I've just taken a statement from an ex-neighbour of Mrs Campion's. It's all about the scarlet daughter – would you like me to read it over?'

'Tell me when she left.'

'Right ... in the November of that year. She had a spat with her mother, if our source is to be relied on.'

'Was she heard of after that?'

'Not by this particular informant. She lived next-door to Mrs Campion until the outbreak of war, after she went to Hayes to the house of her married son.'

'What was the daughter's name?'

'I tried to get it, but she couldn't remember.'

'Was the daughter pregnant at the time?'

'Bless you, yes! Don't you want the details?'

Gently eased his back away from the encroachments of the staircase. The lemonade had re-started his sweat, he could feel drops of it trickling down his brow. Or was the heat entirely responsible ... was some of it due to a different reason? From down the hallway he could hear the vicar in conversation with a tradesman.

'Are you with me? The daughter was married in nineteen-twenty-nine. Her mother disapproved and she wasn't married from home. My informant never saw the man and Mrs Campion never spoke about him – the impression was that he was of the roving kind, or anyway, unrespectable.

'She came back again a year later, not much to the joy of Mrs Campion. The old lady was a bit old-fashioned and her daughter had the reputation of being a man-eater. But the girlie was having a child, which I dare say made a difference; so she duly stayed on and had it – a girl, of course: our old friend Rachel.

'Then there happened this spat between them and the daughter once more slung her hook. She went off in a towering passion, leaving her baby and junk behind her. Her mother thought she'd be coming back for them, but when she didn't, wasn't too surprised. So the baby stayed there and was brought up by its grandmother. It was known from the beginning as Rachel Campion.

'Those are the facts, old man, less the picturesque trimmings. My informant, needless to say, put the least favourable construction on them.'

It had to be the same woman! Gently clutched at his moist receiver. Every detail fitted pat, there wasn't a single trace of discrepancy. And she *had* come back to Hiverton, back to that lonely grave in the marrams. And nobody had missed her at Hiverton. Nobody had missed her at Camden Town.

'Hallo? I want something else done.'

'I could hear you thinking it up.'

'The local police have sent in some dental impressions. I'm pretty well certain that they belong to Rachel's mother.'

'Oh no – don't shove that on to us!'

'Will you see what *you* can do?'

'Why not? The taxpayers expect something for their money. By the way, as you sit there sweating in Northshire...'

Pagram's voice grew suddenly fainter and more distant, and in its place Gently could hear a soft and sibilant drumming. For an instant it grew louder and resembled something familiar; then, as though a switch were pulled, it was cut off entirely.

'Recognize that, old man?'

'Would it be the sound of rain?'

'Rain is right – if you make a habit of the British understatement! The stuff is fairly whirring down. We're in the middle of a freak storm. Over the City way it's as black as ink, and there's a lot of lightning without any thunder. And here's a tip – keep your mac handy: the stuff is heading straight up-country.'

Gently jammed the receiver on its cradle and hurried back to the vicar's den.

'That register... I'd like to see it.'

'Come with me then. It's kept in the vestry.'

Even a townsman could spot it now, the terrific weather that was breeding. The southern sky was all in a haze, and north-ward the landscape as fragile as glass. There was a tense, galvanic stillness. The clamour of a blackbird sounded like a threat. On a distant farm, seeming unable to stop itself, a cock was crowing again and again.

'I could smell this coming all day.'

The vicar was forced to take two strides to Gently's one.

'There was scarcely any dew – did you happen to notice it? In this weather it's a sign that we're going to catch it.'

'I had a feeling, too.'

'Ah! You're country-bred, aren't you?'

'Do you keep the church locked?'

'Good gracious no. Whatever for?'

As he led him up the aisle the vicar gave his chuckle again:

'Talking of that and Bob Hawks puts me in mind of something else. I caught him in here yesterday, and what do you think he was after? The date of his mother's wedding! *If* she was wedded would be more like it!'

'You mean?' Gently caught him by the arm. 'He was in here – *looking at the register?*'

'Just so, as large as life. I had to laugh about it afterwards.'

Gently almost ran into the vestry. The register was lying on a chest of drawers. Quickly he flickered through the pages of life, hope, and mortality. The name stood plump and plain: it was Josephine Rachel Campion. And beside it, like an evil omen, lay a single, tarry thumb mark.

CHAPTER THIRTEEN

He was still nearly running when he got to the beach, but he had known, at every step of the way, that he was making haste too late. His instinct had been right – he should have fastened himself to the Sea-King! It was useless now to pretend that he didn't know how Esau worked.

From the top of the gap, panting, he saw the whole tragic tableau. The rays of the pre-tempest sun drew it in almost psychic luminosity. The sea was as green as grass and the beach shining white. The men on it were as dark brush strokes, the boat, a knifed daub. In the sky, a breathless bowl, there echoed a single, trembling sound: it was the chanting of the motor as the boat put out from shore.

Straight out to sea it was heading, leaving a rulered wake behind it. The surface was now so oily and placid that one could trace every arrowing ripple. Esau was standing to his helm, his upright figure stiff and implacable: he wore no cap over his silvery locks and they lifted slightly in the gentle air. On the beach they were mostly fishermen, but with a sprinkling of hangers-on. All of them were watching silently and in attitudes of bewildered awe.

Gently plunged down the shallow slope, his feet dragging heavily in the sand.

'Ahoy there... Esau Dawes!'

His voice sounded hoarse and futile.

'Ahoy there... *Keep Going!* Ahoy!'

The strange acoustics made the sandhills ring with it. But one might as well have hailed the moon as to hail the departing Sea-King. All the reply was the putter of his engine, growing momently, inexorably fainter. On the air was a whiff of exhaust, on the shingle the print of the keel. Esau had beaten him by five short minutes, but they were as final as five long years.

'It's no good shouting – he won't hear you.'

The fishermen were watching the intruder oddly. Did they know, these alien men, what had made the *Keep Going* put out? Spanton stood there biting his lip. Hawks could hardly get near enough to the sea. Pike, with one or two of the others, was muttering something under his breath.

'But in heaven's name ... why let him do it?'

They had obviously assisted Esau to launch. The blocks, down which the boat had ridden, still lay in position on the beach.

'He said he'd got some business.'

'What – with this lot coming up?'

'You don't ask Esau what he's doing. If he wants to launch, that's up to him.'

But they knew, of course they did: they were showing it like so many children. Without the exchanging of a word they had divined the state of affairs. Esau was launching, and that was enough, they were fishermen and understood. They huddled together in a defensive knot and threw strange glances at the policeman from London.

'Right – then we'll launch another boat.'

There was a shrugging and shaking of heads.

'As a police officer I'm ordering you to give me assistance!'

'What's the use of that, when we couldn't blessed-well catch him?'

It was Pike who volunteered the explanation:

'He's got a Perkins petrol engine aboard her. On a sea like this she'll do eleven knots ... there isn't one of us others can make eight between us.'

'You – Spanton! How much fuel did he

257

have on board?'

'Full tanks.' The young mate didn't bother to look round.

'How far will that take him?'

'To Holland if he wants to go there. But you don't need to worry – he'll never get to Holland.'

'Let him go!' snarled Hawks. 'It's his own affair, isn't it? He knows his own business or nobody can't tell him.'

'The glass has dropped to nothing.'

'He's got eyes in his head! Let him go, I say – what's the sense in bringing him back?'

A gust of hot air whirled suddenly over the beach: it tossed up scraps of litter and hissed spitefully through the marrams. It was followed by a moaning sound, hollow and frightening. The sun was now trapped in a net of the haze.

'You hear that, Jimmy?'

Like blood was the sun. A pulsating ruddy eye, it seemed to boil behind the wrack. To the south the horizon was shuttered under mountains of solid darkness, their outriders advancing with malevolent rapidity. The noose of a hunter! On the glassy lake they were closing, on the clockwork toy that clattered naïvely over its surface.

'It's going to come on a-rummun.'

258

'When you hear the Old Man groan...'

How had the air, from being torrid, grown cold so quickly – as though someone had opened the door of a gigantic refrigerator?

Dutt came plugging over the beach:

'I've brought the car up the track, sir. Inspector Dyson's gone to telephone to Air-Sea Rescue. He took one look down here, sir.'

'Air-Sea Rescue!'

'That's right, sir. From Starmouth. He reckons that they might be able to get here.'

It was the barest of possibilities. The launch could be there in half-an-hour. From Starmouth, by sea, it wasn't more than seven or eight miles. But then they had to get their hands on Esau – and then they had to get home again. And meanwhile, like the wrath of God...

Who could calculate the chances?

'Is this something to do with us, sir?'

The reporters would liked to have known that, too. With their nostrils attuned for a killing, they were watching the event with a dour pertinacity.

'For the moment, I want him back.'

Dutt accepted the hint without pressing his senior. The fishermen, who couldn't have heard what was said, seemed to shrink a little closer in their obstinate huddle. A wind, now hot, now cold, was gusting wailfully up the beach: on the terrible pall to the south a net of lightning had started to flicker.

'You won't see no Air-Sea Rescue!'

They could hear the thunder in distant explosions. The sea had gone black only a few furlongs away, and in a moment the first raindrops were beating on their faces.

'Look at it – ask yourself!'

Hawks was shaking in his glee.

'There ain't nothing going to fetch him – no, not nothing in this world. In a minute it's going to blow like it never blew before!'

'You shut your trap up, Bob!'

Young Spanton had turned on him in a fury.

'Don't you talk like that to me.'

'Shut your trap, or I'll knock you down!'

Hawks's reply was lost in the uproar: the thunder was suddenly over their heads. A whirlwind of rain lashed down on the beach and immediately, it seemed, they were surrounded by darkness. There was a general rush for shelter, though everyone was drenched: it may have been the darkness that sent them all running. Their feet made leprous tracks in the newly-darkened sand, while above them the thunder was sundering the very air.

Somebody had the key to the net store and into this the fishermen tumbled. There was little room inside except what was taken up by gear. The door was slammed and secured with a cord: a hurricane lamp was found and lit. The rain, pelting down on the sheet-iron roof, made a continuous roar between detonations of thunder.

'Damn my hat, but it's a clinker!'

The wind shrieked over the little hut. From its corrugated eaves there were produced a variety of whistlings.

'We won't never beach her again.'

'Nor he'll never get to Holland!'

'Watch your tackle there, old partners – there's a Dutchman got amongst us.'

For they weren't alone in their cluttered den – Gently had managed to squeeze in behind them. A bedraggled figure in his clinging shirt, he stood with his back to the clamouring door. The fishermen silenced themselves directly. Pike, reaching up, trimmed the flickering hurricane. Every second or so it was bleached out by lightning: there was a small, cracked window which faced the sea.

'Robert Hawks! I want to talk to you.'

The lean fisherman glared at him without coming forward. Under the smoky, yellowish light of the hurricane his features looked sharper and unnaturally savage.

'I haven't got nothing to say.'

'Oh yes, I think you have.'

'You know better than me, then!'

'It's to do with Mrs Dawes.'

For an instant the thunder crashed, making any response impossible. Outside a can or something broke loose: it went banging and clattering away up the marrams.

'Mrs Dawes – what's that to do with me?'

Hawks's face had changed, it was sullen and wary. His mates' eyes had faltered from Gently to him – Spanton, especially, was regarding him intently.

'That's what I want to know.'

'I can tell you straight out! I don't know nothing about Esau's missus.'

'*Why did Esau kick her out?*'

'Just you swim out and ask him.'

'I'm asking *you*, Hawks.'

'And I say I don't know!'

Another bout of thunder, lightning sizzling on its tail. The hut blazed and seemed to disintegrate in the white blinding charge. When the glow of the hurricane took over again it showed Hawks, struggling futilely, in Gently's massive grip.

'Once more – I'm asking you!'

'Take your hands off me!'
'Why did he kick her out?'
'How should I know more than the rest!'
Gently struck him across the face. Nobody made an attempt to stop him. A silent, motionless court, they stood like figures in a Dutch interior – a Rembrandt that changed to El Greco when the lightning destroyed the lamp.

'I'll report you–!'
'Answer the question!'
'I tell you straight–'
Gently hit him again. The twisted lips spat blood and showed the teeth in a vicious snarl.

'Some night, when you're not expecting it!'
He aimed a wicked kick at the groin. Gently shortened his grip on the canvas slop and shook the fisherman as though shaking a rat.

'Answer me!'
'How should – don't hit me!'
His teeth were rattling in his head.
'Everyone can tell you – it was to do with other men!'
'Which other men?'
'How should I – don't hit me any more!'
'Why did she come back?'
'She didn't!'

He attempted another kick.

For a moment Gently seemed to be crushing him under the weight of gigantic shoulders. Hawks, driven down on his knees, had his face turned full to the lamp: his eyes were cursing Gently, cursing from the depths of a fathomless hell.

Large eyes ... dark eyes ... eyes crazy with passion!

They were the eyes of Mixer's photograph: they were the eyes of Rachel Campion.

With a motion that echoed Esau's Gently hurled the fellow from him. He fell in a tumbled, heap at the feet of his silent comrades.

'And to think you helped him launch...'

Spanton kicked some loose sand at his face.

The little hut was savaged with lightning: when they could see again, Gently was gone.

He was halted outside the hut by a spectacle of unimaginable grandeur. Leaning against the howling wind, he stared seaward in awed unbelief.

The storm had by this time overrun the entire sky, sealing every horizon with its driving black squadrons. The sea had begun to make and there were breakers pounding the beach. The darkness was so complete that it might as well have been midnight. Excepting at one spot – and that was the phenomenon which astounded him! At about a mile out to sea there was an area of angelic light. Above it the clouds had hollowed into an enormous, twisting cauldron, down which, in slanted lines, the sun was pouring its silver fire.

And there was something in that area! – he sheltered his eyes from the sheeting rain. A fleck, no larger than a tiny white bird, showed where the *Keep Going* was still plugging along. Into the storm centre Esau had put her. He was riding the calm at the heart of the hurricane. The storm, which confounded the hearts of men, was friend and brethren to the white-bearded Sea-King.

Gently hurried down the gap to join the rain-battered Wolseley. Dyson, wearing a borrowed oily, had just arrived from the village.

'No luck with Air-Sea Rescue – Dawes has had it, I'm afraid.'

'Where's the nearest lifeboat station?'

'Castra, but if you're thinking...'

And then, as Gently let in the clutch:

'Where does Dawes come into this business, anyway?'

The nearest phone box was the one by the Beach Stores. It was cascading water, both inside and out. The instrument, at first, sounded dead as a door knocker; then it burst into life with a fizzing of interference.

'Castra Lifeboat Shed.'

He was put through immediately. At the other end it was the cox'n who came on the line.

'Put out in this lot! Do you know what you're asking me?'

'Just listen a moment until I give you the details.'

He explained the circumstances briefly, the cox'n answering him in grunts. At the end he was hung up with curt instructions to wait. Rain was coursing down the panel at the back of the box and from the roof, which appeared to be cracked, a trickle descended on his shoulders.

'Right you are, now I've had a look. I reckon it may be going to clear. If you think your man can hang on for, say, another hour or more...'

'I shall have to come along with you.'

'You! Are you used to these capers?'

'I might be able to persuade him ... anyway, it's a chance I shall have to take.'

It didn't look any clearer as they hissed along the Starmouth Road. Gently was having to use his lights and to hold the car against the buffeting wind. Twice the lightning blazed from the road, apparently right beneath their wheels: he had to brake to a crawl each time until his eyes became readjusted.

'Did Dawes ever marry, by any chance?'

Now Dyson was probing away at the problem. Dutt they had left at Hiverton with a pair of glasses, borrowed from Neal. He was to watch from the coastguard lookout, to which a telephone was still connected. If he observed any change of course he was to pass it on to Castra.

'He'd've been much younger, wouldn't he?'

'Where exactly do we turn?'

'Beyond the church. I was only thinking...'

But he could get nothing out of Gently.

The lifeboat shed was a tall timber structure, its pent roof jutting out firmly above the beach. A shallow ramp led to the lower level, and from the bottom of this blocks were already in position. Gently jammed the car on to a patch of marrams. Nobody appeared to notice their arrival. The sea, breaking heavily on the beach below them, had a tremendous look to the eye of a landsman.

'Come in here a moment, will you?'

They followed a hand that beckoned to them. Inside, under brilliant lights, the big lifeboat towered on its slip. A small tractor with tracks chuffed fussily in a corner and the crew stood by in yellow oilies and gumboots.

'Here ... in here.'

The cox'n led Gently into the office. He was an elderly man with a shrewd, weathered face. He pointed to a chart which lay spread out beneath an anglepoise: for a moment it looked strange and unintelligible to Gently.

'Confound the blessed thunder! Do you see where we are? There's Hiverton, see, and there's the Ness above it. I'd like you to estimate his speed if you can ... if you're right about his course, he's making good east by north...'

He consulted a table, his lips working noiselessly, then he drew two lines with a parallel rule.

'North-east a quarter north made good should fetch him ... he couldn't make more than seven, and we've the wind aft of the beam.'

Gently was hustled into oilies, gumboots and a life jacket. The cox'n poured him a tot of brandy and clinked glasses with ceremony. Dyson stood mournfully by, his opinion in his face. There were limits, it seemed to say, to the proper duties of C.I.D. men.

At the last moment he came forward.

'Under the circumstances, don't you think?'

Gently shrugged and scribbled some notes on the back of a borrowed message form.

'For the background to it get hold of Pagram at the Yard. The rest you can piece together... Simmonds, of course, you needn't detain.'

The launch, when it came, was improbably casual – in point of fact, the sea had not yet risen very high. They were nudged through the breakers with no untoward incident, the clutch was knocked in, and they were surging on their way.

'Go below if you want to.'

The cox'n nodded towards the doorway. Through a couple of fixed ports one could see the lighted cabin.

'If you don't mind I'd sooner...'

'Just suit yourself, of course. But if you want to be sick, anchor your toes under this rail.'

They were striking the seas at an angle and the boat soon took on a roll. Every so often one hammered her and flushed the cockpit with uncomfortable gallons. The shore disappeared as if by magic. One saw it only in the blazes of lightning. For all practical purposes their world was a few acres, capped in by murk and pummelled by the screaming rain squalls.

'Further out they'll come bigger.'

The cox'n seemed to relish the prospect. His eyes rarely strayed from the illuminated compass card. The wheel kicked visibly in his tanned, hairy hands, but each time it was met with a sort of mechanical reflexion.

'And if you want to be sick...'

Why did he have to harp on that? Gently hunched himself uneasily against the white-painted coaming. In the usual way he was quite a good sailor, in his youth he had done the trip to Stockholm in a cargo boat.

Some distance out they changed course, which brought the seas almost astern of them. The lifeboat now had a pitching motion which was very far from happy. Twice she was pooped by curling rollers, rather heavily the second time. Gently, caught on the hop, was partially choked by the torrent of salt water.

'You can always go below.'

But he clung to his post in the cockpit. His experience of past trips had taught him that this was the safest way. The pity of it was that he'd had no food – it always helped, a well-filled stomach. At lunch he'd had nothing but salad, followed by a sickly tasting trifle.

He tried to concentrate on the boat and its thrashing, ponderous motion: but then, almost at the same time, he knew that he'd have to be sick. His stomach and bowels were staging a sudden rebellion, they were snapping away his efforts at conscious control.

'Toes under the rail!'

The rest was unrelieved misery. Before long he had ceased caring about the storm or anything else. After retching he succumbed and tumbled down into the cabin, and there, on a heaving bunk, had wanted nothing but to die.

Later on, it seemed to him that he had been below for hours. He could remember every minute of that pitching inferno. Two of the crew were actually playing cards – they used the engine-casing for a table: a third, cigarette in mouth, was holding down the pile of discards.

'Twist!'

'I'll go a bundle.'

He never found out what it was they were playing. Their absorption in the game lent a crazy touch to the scene. At the end of every hand a copper or two was passed between them. He could have sworn it went on for a week, although his watch said forty minutes.

'Try to drink some of this, old partner.'

They had slopped him out some coffee. A thermos-flask, as big as a barrel, was being tilted over the cup.

'We all get a touch of it, now and then.'

How could the fellow lie to him like that? Gently *knew* that they'd never been seasick: they were a different style in humanity.

Then finally, to end the nightmare, had loomed a dripping figure from the cockpit:

'We've sighted a vessel ahead, sir ... cox'n would like to have you on deck.'

Really, he couldn't have cared less, but he dragged himself up the steps again. Fortunately the tumult he stumbled into had the effect of clearing his brain. It was a good deal lighter, now, and one could see for considerable distances. Behind them, which was southerly, there was a horizon of watery yellow.

'That'll be her, I reckon.'

The cox'n pointed briefly over the fairing. At first Gently could make out nothing except the rolling bulks of waves. Then, as they lifted, he glimpsed it, only a few hundred yards away: it was sliding down a greyback, its varnished counter pointed towards them.

'We'll be up with him very shortly.'

Gently caught a quizzical side glance.

'I know all about old Esau ... what do you

think you're going to do?'

There wasn't any answer to that one. Gently crouched miserably under the bulkhead. He felt abjectly at the mercy of these men of the sea. In his pursuit of the Sea-King he had been lured out of his element, and now, as he closed with him, he was being made to feel the folly of it.

'We can beat him for speed in a seaway like this, but there'll be no going aboard him, if that's the idea.'

'Will I be able to speak to him?'

'You can use the loud hailer.'

'In this ... could she last?'

'He's rode out the worst of it.'

They bullocked closer and closer, rolled on waves like small mountains. Ahead of them the *Keep Going* switchbacked easily over the crests. Esau still stood to his helm, his feet planted a little apart; he swayed to the boat's motion as a circus rider to his horse.

For the cox'n the seas held a clinical interest:

'Up here, we don't often get them this size.'

One of the crew drew attention to the *Keep Going*'s buoyancy:

'He must have a power pump – there's everything on that boat!'

At last they had closed to within fifty or

sixty yards of him: they were near enough to read the gilded lettering on the name board. The cox'n nudged Gently and motioned towards the loud hailer.

'You can call him up now, but we shall have to keep a distance.'

Gently unclipped the instrument, which resembled a clumsy megaphone. Never before had he felt so strongly the futility of what he was going to do. Sick, and feeling weak as a child, he balanced the hailer on the fairing. His knees were cockling under him each time they smacked into a trough.

'Ahoy there, *Keep Going!*'

The wailing voice was not his own: a mournful sea thing, it went protesting through the chaos.

'Esau... ahoy! Can you hear me ... Esau!'

Only a few hours before he'd been making the same appeal to Simmonds.

'Esau ... listen!'

But why should he bother to listen? What was this mewling landsman's voice to the storm-riding Sea-King?

'Esau, as a police officer...'

That was the biggest joke of the lot! He could feel the cox'n's eye running over him, half in irony, half in pity.

'Esau, you have a duty–'

274

Mercifully, he was spared the rest. The Sea-King, till now unmoved, suddenly stirred and reached down beside him: when he straightened up he had something in his hand, and it was something that drew a shout from the cox'n.

'Watch out – he's got his signalling pistol!'

The wheel was twisted through several turns. The result, from Gently's view point, was catastrophic to a degree. From pitching on an even keel the lifeboat staggered into a roll: the man from the Central Office went immediately spinning across the cockpit.

'Everyone ... heads down!'

A roar and a flash accelerated the panic. A scorching blast swept over the cockpit and something hammered against the fairing. The boat seemed trying to bury her side, she was literally on her beam ends. A mountainous wall of sea swept up to obliterate the watery sky.

'My God ... he blew his tank!'

The cox'n heaved at the wheel with all his might. Slowly, like a drunken whale, the lifeboat payed up and righted itself. A sea crashed stunningly over the bows, pouring havoc through the cockpit. A shower of glowing debris hissed into the water near them like shot.

'Look – just look over there!'

Gently dragged himself up to the coaming. Off their port bow the sea was alight, a spreading lake of orange flame. Somehow it was beating the racing seas – had the explosion chopped them flat? – it had made a calm for its writhing tongues, a forcible truce in the turmoil of waters.

'I saw him unscrew the cap!'

They were lurching towards that forest of flame.

'He shoved in the muzzle and pulled the trigger. He still had his other hand fast on the tiller.'

And he was gone, like the wind itself; gone, like a myth of the sea. Nobody was ever to put Esau behind bars: when the shadow reached out, he slipped his moorings and kept going.

'I'll turn in the oil here... there's nothing we can do.'

Grim faced, the cox'n steered into the burning petrol. The object which struck the fairing tumbled off into the cockpit – it was the Sea-King's shattered name board, still attached to a fragment of transom.

Gently stooped to pick it up. And the splinters pierced his finger.

CHAPTER FOURTEEN

The tempest passed away with all the *éclat* that marked its arrival, and at sunset there were twenty minutes exceeding everything that went before. The whole of the sea and the sky were involved in the exhibition. It was as though the spirit of Ruebens had broken loose with an Olympian palette.

The storm bank had retreated northwards and lay now edged with angry crimson. Beneath it stretched a band of neutral colour, raked end to end by soundless lightning. Overhead hung a bulbous formation of cloud. It was flooded with an aerial, golden yellow. To the south rose great banks of purest turquoise, one of them streaked and tongued with scarlet. A panel of clear pea green held the foreground, descending, pink bordered, into cinnamon and umber. Above this the clouds parted on a royal blue sky, its expanse etched over with sheer white fire.

And the sea – how could one believe in that sea? It was divided between a golden lemon and turquoise. The blue that glowed there mocked any description: it was bluer than all the lakes of Italy.

For twenty minutes one could only gaze foolishly, apparently standing at the threshold of heaven. Then it faded almost instantly, as though the artist had done with it: the whole burning fabric turned to the colour of lead.

This ultimate flourish haunted Gently all night. It seemed an acknowledgement and a comment on the tragedy that preceded it. In his fretting mind Esau appeared as supernatural, as a demi-god briefly enlarged from some Valhalla. This had been more than man! He'd had the stamp of a divinity. He hadn't died his death as much as received a translation. Impatient of his hunters he had cast his mortality aside, and the heavens themselves had borne witness to his return.

Over a morning cup of tea the vision lost some of its glamour. There were aspects of the Sea-King which were all too pitifully human. He had been weak with all his virtues, fallible in the midst of strength. He had fallen to a lesser man and carried misfortune into tragedy.

'Hawks – he's the mystery man of the piece.'

It was thus that Gently had prefaced his

remarks to the Wendham super. Stock had arrived soon after breakfast, intent on hearing the minuter details. Dyson's account on the previous evening had succeeded only in whetting his appetite.

'You think he knew that Dawes'd done it?'

'No. I'm fairly certain he didn't.'

'Or that he'd done for his wife?'

'He may have guessed it, but there again...'

They were sitting on the terrace at Gently's favourite spot beneath the oak trees. After the storm the sunlight was brilliant and the air had a liquid sweetness. About them the life of the Bel-Air proceeded – tennis, basking, the strains of a record. The Midlands couple had gone down to the beach and Colonel Morris was now due to appear.

Everything changed but remained the same! Or was it, perhaps, the other way about?

'I'm beginning to get the idea a little clearer. At the same time, judging from what Dyson could tell me...'

'A great deal of it will have to be guesswork.'

'I appreciate that, but I dare say you'll realize...'

'It'll tie-up neatly on the available evidence.'

Gently was wanting to think rather than to talk about the case. It was just the minuter details that no longer interested him. Behind them lay a broader concept, dimly shaping in his brain; it had begun to press upon him as he lay, half-dead, in the lifeboat.

'Hawks was certainly Rachel's father, though we shan't be able to prove it. But there was only one reason why he should want to check the register. He had begun to suspect about Rachel and the register gave proof of identity. Until the episode at the church, I imagine he was still blaming Simmonds for her death.'

'I'd like to get back to Mrs Dawes for a moment.'

'The report on the dentures has settled that one.'

'The identity, yes. But I'd like a little more.'

'As I said, a lot of it will have to be guesswork.'

Yet it was guesswork which lacked every element of doubt: Esau had opened the whole matter to him on those scarifying marrams. He had taken Gently to the grave and had made sure that he grasped its import. In his own inarticulate way he had confessed to the murder of his wife.

'He chucked her out because of Hawks –

again, there won't be any proof. At the time he may not even have known that Hawks was the man in question. They were always having rows, I'm told ... no doubt she threw it up at him. It'd be when she came back that he caught her with Hawks, and that, I believe, was what finally did her business.'

'Why do you suppose she came back?'

'Only Hawks can tell you that. To tell him about his child, perhaps, and to fix up something with him.'

'And Hawks knew what Esau did?'

Gently shrugged. 'Not in my opinion. But he knew that Esau had found out about him and he may have tumbled to the rest. And so it went on, for thirty-odd years.'

For three hundred and ninety fisherman's moons. The boats had gone out and the boats had come home, the skeps had been filled, the nets hung to dry. And on it had festered, that unhealing wound, in the ugly village, by the beautiful shore.

'Campion came here quite by accident?'

'Of that one can be positive. Her grandmother would have told her nothing about Hiverton. The match was disapproved and Mrs Dawes disowned – Rachel took the family name. I expect a suitable tale was told her.'

'Why did Dawes do her in, would you say?'

'Because she was too much like her mother! *He* recognized her directly, almost as soon as he set eyes on her. He part told and part showed me that he'd been spying on her movements.'

'Revenge, too, on Hawks?'

Gently shook his head deliberately. 'If it had been the other way ... but there wasn't any revenge in Esau. No, he was executing the law, the law according to Esau Dawes. Rachel came of a tainted stock, and having sinned, she had to go. Once she'd gone into the tent with Simmonds it was only a matter of time.'

'And then he tried to throw it on Simmonds?'

'I'm not entirely convinced of that. He may have wanted to punish Simmonds – it was Hawks and Mrs Dawes over again.'

Who could tell what'd been going on in the inaccessible mind of the Sea-King? At what point had the deed's consequences come starkly and squarely home to him? Was it when he accosted Gently with the account of Simmonds's thrashing – was it when he saw the artist being hounded off the marrams?

One thing alone was certain: he had faced the consequence unmoved. In the fearless court of his spirit he had first condemned himself to die. And he would have Gently understand him, he wanted the circumstance known in full: this was not the petty violence of a Hawks, a Maurice, or a Mixer.

Yesterday, on the hedge bank, he had sat waiting for Gently to arrest him.

'What do you make of that church business? Dyson told me all about it.'

'At the time it occurred to me...'

How could he explain his tangled ideas? There Esau had made his restitution, he had given Simmonds back his life. Also he had provided Gently with a token which the latter was too dense to perceive. This is not the man, it had said, this is not the one who is to die. The inference was crystal clear ... now, as one looked back on it!

'At the time Hawks thought that Simmonds had done it and he was possessed with a desire for revenge. When the rescue took place he couldn't contain his anger. It was then, I think ... after Esau struck him.'

'He guessed, do you mean?'

'It's impossible to say.'

'He'll be able to guess some more after the inquest on Mrs Dawes!'

The thing you had to remember about this was the sea: in sum, that was Gently's grand conclusion. He'd begun to take it in as he lay on the bunk, as he shrank by the cox'n in the wave-swept cockpit. The sea that was not the land – but more than this, too! The sea that was a life, a separate cosmos on its own. For it possessed a reality that irradiated men's souls: it blinded their understanding to the sobriety of the shore. *There* they refuelled, re-stocked, rested up: *that* could be ugly, penurious, wretched. Their lives only began again when the keel left the beach, when the bows started to rise over the intoxicating waves.

Ashore they watched the sea with vacant, far-searching eyes. Each day they went down to gaze at the element that had bewitched them. To these, what were the shanties and villas of Hiverton, or the ghostly shore people who quarrelled and scolded there?

If one of them offended you, why, you put a stop to it. They were too little real to trouble one's conscience. And if they gathered together and rattled their gallows, to the boat! to the sea! – let them follow if they dared.

Yes, it was the sea that one had to acknowledge, the sea that derided the values of landsmen. Wherever a man went down to it in a boat, there began an allegiance beyond the kenning of cities. The sea had its children and they belonged not to the shore.

284

'Seriously, do you think the old man would have made Holland?'

He could have made the Celebes or far-distant Cathay.

'Well, it's saved a lot of money, the way it's turned out.'

And perhaps something else, even more precious than that.

By a vagary of chance he was to hear some more of Simmonds. The young man went to live in a village in Wiltshire. A relative of his mother's took him in for a time, and it so happened that Gently's married sister lived in the vicinity. The artist had changed his name from Simmonds to Symons. He had given up insurance and was devoting his time to his brush. During the autumn he had held an exhibition in Salisbury, and though he didn't sell many pictures, was at least making an income.

'But he looks a nervous wreck.'

Bridgit's phrase was twice underlined.

'He slinks about the village as though someone was going to bite him. By all accounts he isn't so terribly popular with his aunt – she only puts up with him because of the time he's had.'

In the spring he went off to Cornwall and

Gently lost sight of him.

Hiverton, however, he saw again a year later. He had been called out to Crowlake to give evidence of identification. His way was on the coast road which passed within a mile of the place, and indulging a mild curiosity, he made a detour to take it in. It was just as nondescript as he had remembered it. There was little that was fresh to be discovered. A new sunblind was being sported over the steps to the Beach Stores, another council house or two had been erected down the lane.

He had a pint in the bar of The Longshoreman, where only the publican seemed to recognize him. At their tables the old men still shuffled their dominoes and the fishermen still huddled together in a conclave. There was only one change in the established order. Until he was going out, he failed to notice it. Now it was Hawks who was sitting in Esau's corner, and drinking, from the evidence, one pint after another...

He looked in also on the vicar, who kept open house for everyone, and he found him in his garden tying up some gladioli. He had lately, he said, married off his youngest daughter; now, excepting for his housekeeper, he was living there alone.

286

The publishers hope that this book has given you enjoyable reading. Large Print Books are especially designed to be as easy to see and hold as possible. If you wish a complete list of our books please ask at your local library or write directly to:

Magna Large Print Books
Magna House, Long Preston,
Skipton, North Yorkshire.
BD23 4ND

This Large Print Book, for people
who cannot read normal print,
is published under the auspices of

THE ULVERSCROFT FOUNDATION

... we hope you have enjoyed this book.
Please think for a moment about those
who have worse eyesight than you ...
and are unable to even read or enjoy
Large Print without great difficulty.

You can help them by sending a
donation, large or small, to:

**The Ulverscroft Foundation,
1, The Green, Bradgate Road,
Anstey, Leicestershire, LE7 7FU,
England.**
or request a copy of our brochure for
more details.

The Foundation will use all donations
to assist those people who are visually
impaired and need special attention
with medical research, diagnosis
and treatment.

Thank you very much for your help.